STEVEN SANDOR

JAMES LORIMER & COMPANY LTD., PUBLISHERS
TORONTO

This is a work of fiction. The names, characters, incidents and many locations are
products of the author's imagination. Some elements of the locations used in this
work of fiction are real, but the characters and events described in this book are
entirely fictitious. Any resemblance to actual events, organizations, or persons, living or dead, is coincidental.

James Lorimer & Company Ltd., Publishers acknowledges the support of the
Ontario Arts Council. We acknowledge the support of the Canada Council for the
Arts which last year invested $24.3 million in writing and publishing throughout
Canada. We acknowledge the Government of Ontario through the Ontario Media
Development Corporation's Ontario Book Initiative.

ONTARIO ARTS COUNCIL
CONSEIL DES ARTS DE L'ONTARIO

The Canada Council | Le Conseil des Arts
for the Arts | du Canada

Canadä

Cover design: Meredith Bangay & Tyler Cleroux
Cover image: Shutterstock

Library and Archives Canada Cataloguing in Publication

Sandor, Steven, 1971-, author
          Crack coach / Steven Sandor.

Issued in print and electronic formats.
ISBN 978-1-4594-1000-8 (bound).--ISBN 978-1-4594-0980-4 (pbk).--
ISBN 978-1-4594-0981-1 (epub)

          I. Title.

PS8637.A547C73 2015   jC813'.6   C2015-904206-2
                                                       C2015-904207-0

James Lorimer &	Canadian edition	American edition
Company Ltd., Publishers	(978-1-4594-0980-4)	(978-1-4594-1000-8)
117 Peter St., Suite 304	distributed by:	distributed by:
Toronto, ON, Canada	Formac Lorimer Books	Lerner Publishing Group
M5V 2G9	5502 Atlantic Street	1251 Washington Ave N
www.lorimer.ca	Halifax, NS, Canada	Minneapolis, MN, USA
	B3H 1G4	55401

Printed and bound in Canada.
Manufactured by Friesens Corporation in Altona, Manitoba, Canada in May 2016.
Job #222755

I am a product of two cities; the Greater Toronto area, where I grew up and lived at different stages through my life, and Edmonton, the wonderful city my family now calls home. I'd like to thank the incredibly supportive Edmonton writers' community for their support and feedback.

CHAPTER 1
THE LIST

It was an amazing result. Look, we all expected Bob Jones to win — he had too much support in the suburbs. But it was the margin of victory that stunned the city. In what was supposed to be a four-candidate race, he got over 60 per cent of the vote — the biggest landslide margin in Toronto election history. The other mayoral candidates combined couldn't come close to what Bob Jones did. This was a stunning mandate handed to a man who, as a councillor, voted against the old mayor at every turn. Now, you have to ask: is he the most popular politician Toronto has ever had? Is he the face of our city? And what's next for this man? Provincial politics? Could this be our prime minister one day?

Maurice looked into the mirror; his mouth was foaming with toothpaste. While he stood in the bathroom, he could hear the radio announcer's voice coming from the kitchen, where his mom was brewing coffee and waiting for the bread to come out of a toaster that only sometimes worked.

Maurice put down the toothbrush, rinsed, and then walked out toward the kitchen. His mom had unplugged the toaster, which was smoking. She was trying to pry the bread out of the slot with a fork.

"Looks like I'll skip breakfast," Maurice said, and then he looked at the clock.

"Oh, no! I'll have to skip breakfast anyway! I'm late!"

Maurice raced back into his bedroom, buttoned up his white dress shirt, and wrapped his grey necktie around the collar. Luckily, he knew how to tie a tie in no time flat. He slid into his red cardigan, which had a Loyola Catholic High School crest on the right side, slung his backpack around his shoulders, and raced out the door.

"Bye, Mom!"

The elevator ride to the lobby seemed so agonizingly slow. Maurice then dashed through the front door, onto the street, and to the closest bus stop on Dixon Road.

And then he waited. Maurice looked up at the sky. Piercing screams of jet engines filled the air; they competed with the cranked-up bass line coming through his headphones. Even with the music turned up to almost full blast, Maurice couldn't completely shut out the *whhhheeeeeeeee* of the jets coming from overhead.

Maurice wondered how the plane, despite going hundreds of kilometres an hour, could look like it was almost frozen in the air. It was close enough to the ground to cast a large shadow on the street as it headed toward the airport. The runways were only a few blocks away — just across the many busy lanes of Highway 401 that separated Pearson Airport from the nearby Etobicoke neighbourhoods. The highway was like a concrete barrier loaded with grumbling trucks and cars and buses that kept the edges of his neighbourhood from butting right against the runway fences.

Maurice took his eyes off the sky and looked down the street. A steady stream of cars passed the bus shelter, but there was no red, white, and black bus. Maurice sighed. He'd been at the shelter for at least fifteen minutes.

In his mind, he was at a crossroads. *If I start walking to school, it'll take me about half an hour. Or I'll keep waiting. And who knows when the bus will come? Either way, I'll be late.*

Maurice sighed. *I could always run a few blocks to make up some time — even though, being a teenager on a dead run in this neighbourhood, I could end up getting picked up by the cops. No matter the time of day.*

But he knew that simply wasting precious minutes at the bus shelter would only guarantee he'd be late. The problem with Toronto buses was that they seemed to not follow any sort of schedule; three buses could go by in the span of five minutes, then half an hour might pass before the next one showed. So Maurice picked up his red school bag from the sidewalk and took a few steps away from the bus shelter. But as he looked back one last time, he spotted a red, white, and black rectangular shape in the distance.

Isn't it always like this? Maurice thought. *As soon as you give up on the bus, it shows up.*

He jogged back to the stop. The red rectangle grew larger and larger. It slowed and stopped in front of him.

On the side of the bus was an ad that featured a picture of Bob Jones — or Coach Jones, as he was known to every football player at Loyola Catholic High School. His smile was wide, from puffy cheek to puffy cheek. Next to Jones's face was the slogan: "Stop the Waste."

Maurice flashed his pass to the driver. The bus was full, and there were no seats available. Commuters crowded into the aisle. Maurice stood next to a woman whose belly ballooned out — even though she was obviously pregnant, no one had gotten up to offer her a seat.

He looked out the window and saw front lawn after front lawn go by. Coach Jones's signs and slogans were still on most of them. The bus rocked to the left and right. Maurice held on tightly — he didn't want to stumble and bump the mom-to-be next to him.

I wonder how long after the election we'll still be seeing the signs, Maurice wondered.

He saw so many of Jones's signs, he couldn't even dream of counting them in his head. They had slogans like:

"Working Hard to Get Great Results!" (Coach used that one in practice a lot.)

"Integrity, Not a Cash Grab."

"Stop the Waste."

As the bus waited to make a left turn at a stoplight, Maurice spotted a large cardboard placard perched in a front window: "This is Etobicoke. We are all Bob Jones."

At the next bus stop, two women got on. Even though it was September, the hot, sticky summer hadn't let go of

Toronto. A person would only need to stand outside for a couple of minutes before being covered in sweat. But the two women, who flashed their Metropass cards at the driver, wore black jackets and long shawls over their heads. Maurice smiled when he saw the series of buttons pinned to their coats, each reading "JONES NATION."

The person sitting next to Maurice had the *Toronto Sun*'s front page displayed on his iPad. On the screen was a picture of Coach Jones, a microphone in his hands. "Landslide!" read the headline.

The bus pulled up to the stop in front of the high school. Maurice looked at his cell-phone clock. *I'm in luck — I have five minutes to make homeroom.* He dashed down the bus steps, out the door, and made a beeline for the front entrance. He had already earned three late slips over the last two weeks, and he knew that adding another one could affect his academic standing. As well, the final cuts for the football team were supposed to be posted outside the athletic office that morning, and Maurice wondered if he'd have enough time to make the detour before he had to be in homeroom.

As he raced toward the school, the doors opened in front of him. He ran right into a group of Grade 12s, who were walking out to the portable classrooms.

"Watch where you're going, Minor Niner!" one of them hissed at Maurice. Even though Maurice was already six feet tall and could see eye-to-eye with the older student, he slumped his shoulders and looked down at the ground. "Sorry," he mumbled.

"You better be, Minor Niner!"

But someone else from the group spoke up. She elbowed the guy who had just threatened Maurice.

"You idiot! Don't you know who that is? That's The Streak's kid brother!"

"What?"

"The Streak! He has a little brother! And you just lipped him off!"

The guy who had yelled at Maurice put his arms up. "I'm sorry. I didn't know." It was his turn to slump his shoulders and stare at the ground.

Maurice shrugged and went through the doors. As soon as he got inside, he was sucked up into a noisy wave of humanity. Students going in every direction jostled each other and talked.

There were girls spraying their hair and safety-pinning up the skirts of their school uniforms, goth kids putting on their eyeliner, preppy boys fixing their neckties. Other guys wore their white dress shirts open-collared, the red school cardigan hanging off their shoulders. Despite leaving the apartment in a rush, Maurice had his collar done up tight and crisp; he'd learned a Windsor knot in front of a mirror so his necktie would look as classy as possible. He knew that his strict adherence to the uniform was the calling card of a Minor Niner, but there was no way his mom would allow him to leave the apartment if he had an open collar or had rolled up the sleeves of his dress shirt.

Maurice dodged and darted through his schoolmates as if they were tacklers on the football field. He got to his locker and opened the door. There was a blue letter M bordered in yellow — the logo of the University of

Michigan Wolverines — stuck to the inside of the locker door, just above the little stick-on mirror.

Maurice drew his smartphone out of his pocket and looked at the time. He now had just one minute to make it to his first class. The hard soles of his dress shoes allowed him to skid through the hallway, where he crashed into a tall, skinny teen who was headed the same way as Maurice.

"Veee-jayyy!" Maurice called out.

"Easy, man," Vijay Panesar threw out his arm behind Maurice's back, making sure his friend wouldn't fall over. Maurice weighed more than 180 pounds. For Vijay, who might have weighed 130 pounds soaking wet, helping Maurice keep his balance was a true test of strength.

Maurice's feet finally gained some traction. "Not as good on these dress shoes as I am on cleats," he said. "And it sucks because we don't have time to check if the final cuts were posted."

Vijay smiled. "You mean that *you* didn't have the time to check. Unlike someone who will remain nameless, *I* got to school with a few minutes to spare. And I saw the cuts."

"What!" Maurice grabbed his friend by the shoulders. "And? And? And?"

"Come on. You make it sound like you weren't a sure thing. Your name was on the top of the team list. A Grade 9 was listed above all the Grade 10s."

"Yes!" Maurice pumped his fists. Then he paused and took a deep breath. "What about you?"

"Much to my surprise, I was on the team list. The very last name. But I was on it!"

"All right!" Maurice cheered.

The pair high-fived each other and walked through the door of their classroom just as the bell rang. They hurried to sit at their desks, which were right next to each other.

They stood with their classmates as the national anthem came across the PA system. As O Canada came to its final crescendo, Maurice felt a buzz coming from his pants pocket. His phone!

Prayers were next; Father O'Halloran's robotic rendition of the "Our Father" filled the speakers. Mr. Cangelosi, the homeroom teacher, was staring intently at the cross that hung above the chalkboard at the front of the room. It was like he was in a trance. But more importantly, he wasn't looking at the class. Maurice took the chance to snatch his phone from his pocket and look at the text message on the screen. It was from his mother.

DID U MAKE IT?

Maurice gulped and stuffed the phone back in his pocket just before Mr. Cangelosi turned around.

After the Lord's Prayer came the Hail Mary. And Father O'Halloran made sure every word was uttered slowly and clearly, in monotone. As everyone stood, Maurice couldn't help but shuffle his feet impatiently, making scraping noises on the floor.

Vijay punched Maurice in the shoulder.

Finally, the prayer came to an end. Maurice crossed himself, like every other student in the class except for Vijay — who wasn't Catholic despite the fact he went to a Catholic high school. Father O'Halloran made a comment about how some girls were "hiking up their kilts too high."

It seems like he says that every couple of days, Maurice thought to himself. *And every week he threatens to change the dress code so the girls have to wear slacks or long skirts. And it never happens. The school is the one that made the plaid skirts part of the uniform — why does Father need to point it out all the time, then?*

The principal came on and Maurice tuned out. He knew to listen for his name; if he didn't hear it, what the principal said likely didn't concern him.

Then, silence. Announcements over.

Finally, Maurice thought.

He shot his hand into the air. "Mr. Cangelosi! Sir!"

Mr. Cangelosi, who was about to write something on the board, turned and looked at Maurice. "Yes, Mr. Dumars?"

"I need to be excused for a minute," Maurice said.

"Mr. Dumars, class has only just begun."

"Um, it's urgent. Really urgent. I have an urgent family issue."

"Yes, Mr. Dumars, the *urgency* of your situation is clear to me."

Maurice heard snickers from some of his classmates.

"Please, sir?"

Mr. Cangelosi sighed. "Very well. I expect that this, ahem, *urgent* matter won't require you to miss class entirely?"

"No, sir. Just five minutes!"

Mr. Cangelosi walked to the classroom door and opened it. "Five minutes, then."

Maurice walked out of the class and into the hall. As

soon as he was away from the door, the walk turned into a jog, even though he slipped once or twice in his dress shoes. He arrived at the nearest men's room and slipped inside.

He fished his phone out of his pocket and texted:

MADE IT!!!

He waited to see if a response bubble would form right away. It did.

OK!!! I'LL LET FABIEN KNOW

Maurice leaped into the air. He felt dizzy. He closed his eyes and imagined himself wearing the red Loyola football jersey. Then he thought even harder and imagined he was wearing the blue and yellow of the University of Michigan! The Wolverines! Just like Fabien! One of the greatest teams in all of college football! On TV every weekend!

The buzz from his phone interrupted his wonderful daydream.

MAURICE, YOU THERE? YOU OK?

YEAH. HERE. THANKYOUTHANKYOU THANKYOUTHANKYOU

LUV U!!! CELEBRATE 2NIGHT AFTER WORK!!!

Maurice put the phone back in his pocket. Now he

had to get back to his homeroom. And, somehow, he had to manage to pay attention and not dream about playing football during class. He looked into the mirror just as the washroom door opened. Two older teens, shirts unbuttoned enough so you could see their T-shirts underneath, walked in.

"Today is the greatest day of my life! Thank you!" Maurice howled at them.

"Man, the niners are especially weird this year," one of the boys said to the other.

CHAPTER 2
MEET THE NEW MAYOR

Maurice sat on a bench in the boys' change room, which also doubled as the dressing room for the school football team. He scrolled through the newsfeed on his smartphone.

"WILL HE OR WON'T HE?" read the headline. Maurice clicked on the icon so he could read the story.

> TORONTO (CP) — Less than twenty-four hours after receiving a mandate from the people of Toronto, Mayor-Elect Bob Jones will see his priorities put to the test.
>
> When asked if he would be attending tonight's meet-the-candidates dinner with the Gay and Lesbian Alliance, Jones told reporters that he would instead be in Etobicoke, running practice for the Loyola Catholic High School's junior football

team. Jones, who graduated from that high school thirty-two years ago, has been a volunteer coach for the team for the last five years.

"My voters understand how important it is to me to be out in the community, and that means coaching the football team," Jones said.

But Gay and Lesbian Alliance Executive Director Beth Grieves said if Mayor-Elect Jones won't attend the dinner, it will send a "sobering message" to her community.

"He's already made a habit of ignoring us; if he chooses a couple of hours of high school football over our community, it only echoes his previous actions."

Grieves referred to Jones's decision to skip the City's annual Pride festival across each of the eight years in which he served as a councilor for his Etobicoke ward.

Maurice heard a door swing open, followed by heavy footfalls. He quickly darkened his phone's screen as Coach Bob Jones, the man himself, appeared.

"You ready to get out there, champ?" Coach Jones asked. His face was red and round, like an overripe tomato. It was hard to tell if he had a neck or not. He wore a hooded sweatshirt that had JONES NATION written on it.

The rest of the team had already left the dressing room and headed out to the field for practice. But Coach Jones had asked Maurice to stay behind for a second.

"I'm ready, Coach," Maurice said. "Focused. I want to

make you proud of me. You can work me into the lineup wherever you can. I know that I'm just a niner and won't get to play every down."

"Are you kidding?" Coach Jones smiled and squinted. In fact, he squinted every time he smiled. "As soon as I saw you at the first practice, I knew that you'd be a big part of this year's team. Really, you remind me so much of Fabien. And you, of all people, know how long I worked with your brother. I helped build him up. I helped make him a man. I tried to be the father figure he didn't have — like you don't have."

Awkward, thought Maurice. But he decided against saying anything.

"Maurice, I've known you and your brother for a long time. The Streak was one of the hardest-working kids I've ever worked with. I remember him playing junior football on this team. And, heck, when we graduated him to the senior team I just knew he'd set every school rushing record. And he did. I helped get him to Michigan. I might be the coach, a boring old white guy from the nice part of the neighbourhood, but I can understand what it's like to be a black kid from the not-so-nice part of this hood. You have to be that one hardest-working kid who makes it. Period. I just wanted to say, congratulations. You've earned it."

Coach put an arm on Maurice's shoulder pad. Had Coach Jones just wiped a tear from his eye? Maurice took in a deep breath through his nose, and caught the sharp smell of orange mouthwash from the coach. Or *was* it orange mouthwash? It was sweet and powerful.

Wait, thought Maurice. *Is that whisky?* Maurice had never sipped a drop of the stuff, but he'd smelled it on some of the homeless people camped out on blankets and ratty sleeping bags at the entrance to Islington subway station.

"See, look at you — like me, we're from the hood! Mad skills! I may be a white old man, but I'm your brother!"

Maurice looked at the floor, trying not to grimace. *Here we go again with the race thing. I remember him talking to my brother like this. Why does Coach do this?*

"Maurice, I didn't hear you. Am I your brother?"

Please make it stop. "Yes, Coach," Maurice mumbled.

"Now, let's go kick some ass!" Coach Jones roared.

Coach and Maurice walked out of the dressing room, out of the school, and toward the practice field.

Maurice spotted a cluster of vans parked near one of the end zones. CTV. Citytv. CBC. Global. The CTV van had an antenna sticking straight out of its roof. Around the vans stood a cadre of reporters with notebooks and voice recorders, along with cameramen and a few other people with microphones.

When Coach Jones and Maurice reached the sidelines, the reporters and cameramen converged around them. In what felt like an instant, they were surrounded. Microphones were shoved into Coach Jones's face.

"Mayor-Elect Jones, Mayor-Elect Jones!"

"We have questions!"

"Excuse me, can you tell us why you decided to be here rather than be at the Gay and Lesbian Alliance's 'Welcome new City Council' event?"

"Why are you here rather than attending to business as our new mayor-to-be?"

Coach Jones put up his hand.

"I'm sorry, ladies and gentlemen. I am a football coach at this moment. I am dedicated to these kids and football and, if some people have a problem with that, well, I can promise them that this won't affect my performance as mayor of this town. I'm helping kids. What could be a greater civic responsibility?"

A reporter shouted, "Still, avoiding the Gay and Lesbian Alliance event will allow your fellow council members to call you homophobic —"

"Wait a second!" Coach Jones's red face became, somehow, a little bit redder. "I never said I have a problem with gays or lesbians. All I said is that I also coach football and I made a promise to these kids that I have to keep. Don't dare say I am avoiding that forum. I'm not avoiding it. I have other commitments. If they hold that event on any other night, I'm there."

"Would you sign the declaration recognizing Gay Pride's importance to Toronto?"

"No comment."

"Will you give up football?"

Coach Jones stopped and searched for the owner of the voice. He found the reporter and looked him in the eye. "Of course not. There is no conflict. This kid right here, he should be the one you're interviewing. You remember Fabien Dumars, the Loyola Streak? The kid I sent to Michigan? Well, this is his brother! And I can tell you, he's gonna be every bit as good as The Streak. And he's from our hood! You have any idea what that means to me? Why would I want to stop working with these great kids from this community? How would me being mayor not allow me to keep coaching? When I get sworn in as mayor next week, they won't be asking me to swear to stop coaching football. I never promised in the election campaign that I'd stop coaching football."

Maurice tried to edge his way out of the scrum. Despite the coach's efforts to thrust him into the spotlight, Maurice knew that no one there wanted to talk to him. It was all about Coach Jones and the election he'd just won.

Maurice freed himself from the tangle of mic cables and continued, unnoticed by the media, to the practice field. He saw Vijay catching a few lazy tosses from the starting quarterback.

Vijay turned around. "So, did any of the reporters want to talk to you?"

"You kidding me?" Maurice shrugged. "It's all about the election. Mayor Jones this and Mayor Jones that . . ."

". . . And we'll get coverage of junior high school football games like no other junior high school team has ever got before. Think about it. It's good for us, really, Maurice."

"I guess so."

"Look, what do you have to worry about? You were on the top of the team sheet. You're going to be the star of this team, niner or not."

"Yeah, I just talked to the coach and I think he has big plans for me."

"What's that?" came another voice.

Maurice and Vijay spun to see who had spoken. They saw André Willis, the Grade 10 running back, walking slowly toward them. "Big plans? Better not be any big plans. I sat on the bench in my niner year and only got garbage minutes, knowing I could be the starter this year. Everyone knows that a niner has to pay his dues, no matter who his brother is."

He walked forward and put his finger right between the numbers of Maurice's jersey. "Speaking of your big brother, I see you're wearing his number. Number 28. I'm just laying it out for you now: You better not steal my chance to be the starter just because your brother was a big man here."

Maurice opened his mouth, but before any words could come out, Vijay was already talking back.

"Um, did you watch Maurice in practice last week? He ran circles around you!"

"You should shut up," André glared at Vijay. "We all know why *you* made the team. I saw you at practice last week, and you sucked. Your hands could be sticky like Spider-Man's and you'd still find a way to drop anything that's thrown your way. But you got the sympathy vote from the coach because of your dead cousin or brother or whatever. Good for you."

Vijay's eyes opened wide.

If I punch André in the jaw, will Coach Jones do anything to me? wondered Maurice.

But before Maurice could act, he was interrupted by the hubbub that was created by Coach Jones breaking through the scrum of reporters, like a running back plunging through a defensive line. Jones stormed to the middle of the field, where he was joined by his assistant, Massimo DeAngelis, who was also one of the school's math teachers.

The cameramen and people holding microphones ringed the field.

"Gentle-MEN!" Coach yelled. "Gather round!"

"You heard the coach!" hollered Mr. DeAngelis. "Let's go, move! You, Mr. Panesar. I see you, hustle! I hope you can run faster than you solve problems in my class!"

The team jogged to the middle of the field and stood in front of the coach. Coach Jones looked at the forty players before him.

"I know the last couple of weeks we've had lots of distractions," said Coach. "And some of it is on me. You know that I've been running practices, but also running for election. But we've made it through, so far. And now that big vote is behind me. Remember to thank all of your families for me. But now, we have a big game coming up next week. And I wanted to tell you all something."

The coach took a deep breath. Flashes went off in his face. The clicking noises of cameras followed.

"Gentlemen, you know what I want to win, more than anything? ANYTHING? Well, believe me when I say this: If you gave me a choice between the mayor's office and winning the league, I'd choose the league. You boys, you are special to me. We can achieve great things together. I know some of your moms and dads, sisters and brothers, aunts and uncles. And we are going to show them what this school is all about!"

The boys cheered. All except for Maurice. He saw some of the reporters furiously scribbling in their notebooks.

An hour later, the *Toronto Scene* website had a new front-page story.

PRIORITIES
By Harmon Mcaffee

Our mayor is supposed to represent the whole of our city. He or she is supposed to look after our best interests, no matter the colour of our skin or our sexual orientation.

We don't elect a mayor to be a football coach.

Or, maybe we DID elect our mayor to be a football coach. Because that's where Bob Jones was earlier tonight; instead of meeting with members of the LGBT community, he chose to lead a small group of teens through football practice.

There will be many practices this season. There may be, at best, forty kids on his football team. There are hundreds of thousands of people in Toronto's LGBT community.

Mayor-Elect Jones says he's not homophobic. But he continually decides to ignore the LGBT community. Is he angry because the Gay Village is one of the few places where he did poorly on election day?

Our new mayor has to ALWAYS put the city first. And if it means taking a step away from football, so be it. It's time for him to punt himself off the team.

COMMENTS

Trog1278
You kidden me . . . 1 day after da vote and yer already after Mayor Jones. He's my boy. JONES NATION!

EtobicokeKING
Mamby-pamby liberal crap.

JohnXV
So, you think it's "liberal crap" to ask our mayor to respect all of his citizens? Is this what you voted for? A mayor who will divide our city? Is this OK with you?

EtobicokeKING
And who's trapped our mayor? Scheduling this "event" one day after the election? Of course he might have other plans!

RationalYOUTH
Yup. Big plans. High-school football. Go get 'em.

JonesNATIONRULEZ
Nice 2 see youre all turning the fact that Jones has been coaching football for years, helping kids and all that, into a big nega-TIVE. Nice, Toronto. You don't deserve Bob.

JohnXV
@ JonesNATIONRULEZ: You're right. We don't.

CHAPTER 3
PULLING UP THE SIGNS

Vijay got off the bus and walked toward home. He turned away from Martin Grove Drive and strolled two blocks into the subdivision until he got to Waterbury Drive.

Earlier in the day, in his social studies class, Miss York said people had just three days after the election to get the signs off their lawns.

During his walk, Vijay counted seventeen Bob Jones signs on front lawns.

A lot of people aren't gonna make that deadline, he thought.

He also noticed a series of yellow handbills that were taped to several of the lampposts on his route home. He stopped to look at one.

CRIME REDUCTION STRATEGY SESSION

Come out and join members of the Toronto Police to talk about what we can do to reduce violent crime in 23 Division!

Learn how to be vigilant about gang activity in your neighbourhood! Join us at Centennial Recreation Centre! Learn how to work to make your community safer! Make sure your voice is heard!

The notice showed a map of north Etobicoke, including Vijay's neighbourhood. On the map were about two dozen dots. Each dot represented a shooting that had been reported to police over the past twelve months.

Vijay stopped reading and resumed his walk. *So, that's it huh?* he thought to himself. *Ronny is now just a red dot on a map.* Vijay got to his front yard and saw his dad crouched down, grunting as he yanked and yanked on one of the five Bob Jones signs that still covered the property.

"Progress, Dad," Vijay said as he walked up the driveway. "This morning, there were eight signs on the lawn."

His dad, head slick with sweat, had a white shirt on, with BOB JONES FOR MAYOR in bright purple print. With one last mighty heave, the sign that read BOB JONES: NO MORE PERKS was pulled free of the ground.

"Let me help, Dad," Vijay said. "I can grab that for you and bring it to the trash back there."

Mr. Panesar shook his head furiously. "No, not in the trash."

"Oh, this can go in the recycling bin, instead?"

"No, Vijay," his dad said. "The sign is not trash. It is not for recycling. It is a souvenir! If you want to put it anywhere, put it in the garage. I've started a pile there. I'm keeping them. The law says I have to clear them from my lawn after election day, but it doesn't say anything about me having them in the garage. Huh?"

Vijay bent over and picked up the sign. "Um, Dad, why are we turning our garage into the Temple of Coach Jones?"

His dad was already pulling out another sign, one that read: BOB JONES: A MAYOR WE CAN AFFORD.

"Son, these signs will remind us how we worked to get one of our own elected as mayor. Bob Jones isn't just the football coach at Loyola. He's a man like me and our neighbours. Not some downtown lawyer or some lifetime politician. When he was a city councilor, he'd take a complaint that came from a plumber or a bus driver and then bring it up at City Hall."

Vijay shrugged and walked up the driveway, toward the garage door.

"Son," Mr. Panesar called.

Vijay stopped. "Dad?"

"Look, I know this might seem funny to you; but you have to remember that I've spent a lot of time working on the campaign. Getting Bob Jones elected was so important to this family."

"Dad, of course I know how much this meant to you. After all, you took three weeks vacation so you could work for Mr. Jones. I guess we won't be driving to Florida this year."

"A sacrifice we're happy to make, right?" Mr. Panesar smiled. "Well, I just wanted to remind you that this was important. Bob Jones was the only candidate who promised more money for the police."

"And cut taxes at the same time. Yeah, we talked about it in social studies."

"If we had more cops, maybe Ronny . . ."

Mr. Panesar's voice trailed off. He looked out toward the street, so he missed that his son had rolled his eyes.

"Dad, we've been over this. I know it hurts, but I don't think a few extra cops would have helped Ronny."

"He was a good kid. He was alone that night. He didn't deserve what happened to him."

"Dad, he was alone in a parking lot at 3 a.m. He was waiting for someone; you don't just wait in a Weston parking lot in the middle of a weeknight because you've got nothing better to do. He'd already been suspended from school. He'd been arrested a couple of times. Uncle Rishi had already threatened to kick him out of their house."

"He was such a good kid. When you two were little, you were inseparable. More like twin brothers than cousins."

"Yeah, well, Dad, things change."

Vijay got to the keypad near the garage door, entered the code and waited for the door to open. He tossed the sign in a pile with the others, and then headed into the house.

After passing through the front door he set his bag against the wall, just below the little altar to Ronny that hung in the hallway. In the photo, Ronny was young, smiling. He had a Toronto Blue Jays cap on. Below the picture, on a small shelf, was a lone burning candle.

Vijay walked into the kitchen, where his mom supervised a pot of stew that was bubbling on the stove. A tablet computer was propped up against the sugar and cookie jars, where the kitchen counter met the tiled wall.

Vijay's mom motioned to the screen. "I am waiting for the six o'clock news. Maybe we'll see you. I heard on the radio that all the reporters were at practice!"

"Um, Mom, they don't go there to talk to me."

"Don't you worry," his mom said. "You will all be famous soon. Your coach is going to be sworn in as mayor!"

Vijay walked into the living room, and saw three boxes sitting on the couch. The flaps were open, so he could see what was inside — flyers that read:

CELEBRATE BOB JONES — OUR NEW MAYOR!

PARTY AT ALBION ROAD YMCA! FOR ALL OF OUR CAMPAIGNERS AND SUPPORTERS! THANKS FOR A JOB WELL DONE!

"Um, Mom," Vijay called out. "When did we get these invites?"

"Oh, they came last week. Your dad planned ahead and reserved the hall and had the invitations printed last week. He's going to start handing them out around the neighbourhood tomorrow."

"How much vacation time did Dad have banked? He's got more time off to do all of this?"

"Yes, and I'll be helping him. So I'm going to be swamped this week. You might need to take something out of the freezer for dinner tomorrow."

"Okay, Mom. But you're telling me dad had these printed *before* Coach Jones won the election?"

"Of course! We've been going out and talking to the people. We've done that for months to help this campaign. We knew Bob Jones was going to win."

Vijay's mom put up her hand. "Okay, news is almost on!"

The flat-screen in the corner went purple, and then came the "EVENING NEWS" logo flashing across the screen.

A commentator wearing a plain grey suit, sitting behind a news desk, came on screen.

"Tonight, the temperature rises in Toronto. One day into the job and our mayor-to-be is already in the midst of a controversy. Let's go live to Loyola Catholic High School in Etobicoke, where our own city-affairs reporter, Nadine Kim, was on the scene with Bob Jones — the man who would rather be coaching than leading this city, it seems."

Vijay's mom grabbed a pepper, placed it on the counter, and then brought a knife crashing right down the middle of it.

The screen now showed the reporter standing on the sidelines of the Loyola School field.

"Thanks, Scott. I'm here in Etobicoke, on the Loyola School football field, a place that's very special to Mayor-Elect Jones. So special in fact, that he would rather be here than meeting with Toronto's Gay and Lesbian Alliance, the leadership of which was hoping to meet the mayor tonight. But Scott, we may need to get used to a mayor that puts the gridiron before government."

The scene cut to Bob Jones, speaking into the reporters' microphones: "I am dedicated to these kids and football and, if some people have a problem with that, well, I can promise them that this won't affect my performance as mayor of this town. I'm helping kids. What could be a greater civic responsibility?"

And then Nadine Kim was back on screen. "After meeting with reporters on the football field — and after we were told the mayor-elect would not be available at City Hall today — we then watched as Mayor-Elect Jones told his team that his top priority was to win a football championship for the high school. For those who voted for the mayor to improve transit, police, and lower taxes, they may now be wondering where Bob Jones's priorities lie, just a day after the election. For Evening News, I'm Nadine Kim."

Vijay's mom walked over to the screen and turned it off. "Embarrassing."

"Yeah," Vijay said. "Maybe Coach should have gone to that meeting."

Vijay's mother spun quickly so she could face her son.

"No, embarrassing for that reporter. To already be trying to spread all this muck about the mayor. He's such a good man and I am so proud he is also coaching my son. It's a good thing your father is still outside and did not see it."

CHAPTER 4
SINGLED OUT

The boys sat on the practice field. It was so quiet that the players could hear the music bleeding out of the headphones worn by a nearby jogger.

Maurice didn't know what to say. He felt the eyes of most of his teammates burning through him. That is, except for Vijay. Maurice didn't want to look behind him, because that's where André was standing.

Over the last week, Maurice had dreamed that Coach Jones would name him the starting running back for the season opener. He had memorized the playbook. He finished his wind sprints before anyone else on the team. He hopped through countless tires.

But at every turn, André was right behind him — telling Maurice that he wasn't good enough, that he was nowhere near the player his big brother was.

And all this drama played out in front of the cameras. At

least, in front of cameras that weren't pointed at the players. When practice began, the reporters and camera crews gathered at the sideline. At the end of every practice, the reporters packed around Coach Jones.

But in all the stories that Maurice read or in the news reports he watched on TV, none mentioned any of the players on the team.

There was one photo and report that Maurice had saved on his phone. It was of Coach Jones giving a speech to the Toronto Economist Club; the coach had his red Loyola ball cap on his head.

COACH/MAYOR-ELECT GOES FROM PRACTICE TO POLITICS

Bob Jones is just days away from being sworn in as the Mayor of Toronto, but he remains fiercely loyal to the high-school football team he coaches.

Jones created a stir when he spoke to Toronto's top business people last night at the Economist Club. The black-tie affair saw some of the city's CEOs and financial leaders paying $1,000 a plate for the dinner and the chance to hear the incoming mayor speak about his plans for the city.

But it wasn't what Bob Jones had to say that caught the attention of everyone at the event; it was how he chose to dress. At a black-tie affair, he appeared as if it was Casual Friday: he wore a jacket over a polo shirt, and had a red Loyola High School team hat on his head.

"I just came from my team's practice, and I think we can win it all, just like I can be a winner for you, the Toronto entrepreneur," he said.

I think it's kinda cool that Coach Jones represented at this stuffy event, Maurice thought. Of course, he'd never dream of saying that to his mom, who wouldn't let Maurice leave the house if his necktie wasn't knotted tightly and his shirt wasn't crisply ironed and tucked in.

After each practice, André and many of the other Loyola players would head out to the local patty shop or noodle house. Maurice and Vijay were never invited.

"Minor Niners have to make sure the dressing room is nice and clean," André had said after one practice, smashing his cleats against the dressing-room wall to remove the caked-on mud. "Oh, silly me."

Maurice knew that he should feel like all of the misery André was putting him through was worth it — but he didn't feel any joy.

It all led up to the most-anticipated practice of the season, at least so far. Before practice began, most of the players had been quiet in the dressing room — that is, except for André. The boys knew that Coach Jones would be announcing the starters for the season opener; and André was already celebrating.

"I can't wait to get on the field. No Minor Niner is going to upstage me! You enjoy sitting down on the bench there, Dumars. You'll understand that a niner has to pay his dues!"

On the field, Coach Jones announced the names of the

starting quarterback and wide receivers, and each name was greeted by a loud roar. But the mood changed — as soon as Coach Jones made the announcement on who would start at running back: "Here's the news, boys. Maurice is going to be our starter." There were no cheers. The heads of the players turned to André, whose eyes were bugged almost right out of their sockets. They then all turned to Maurice.

As Maurice sat there, reeling in shock at the announcement, André's voice, hissing into his ears brought him back to Earth.

"Congratulations. I hope your big brother is proud. You can go off and tell him how good you did."

Coach Jones looked up from his clipboard and glanced at Coach DeAngelis, who was standing off to the side. Coach DeAngelis shrugged.

"Excuse me boys," Coach said. "I don't really see any team spirit, there. So let me try this again. I'm proud to say Maurice Dumars will start Friday night's game at running back."

This time, there was a half-hearted round of applause.

Coach Jones took a deep breath. And then another. Then, he hurled the clipboard. It spun in the air and crashed about fifteen yards downfield. Papers scattered everywhere.

"So, I guess you boys all have a problem!" he roared. His face turned red. And then he began to yell even louder. "So, you don't like Maurice, huh? Is this because you all think that I'm giving him the job because he's The Streak's brother? Is that it?!"

The team was quiet again.

"Okay, then. If you've got a problem with that choice, you bring it to me. You don't go and embarrass Maurice like that. Making him the starter was my decision. You're all welcome to meet me after practice at the athletic office and you can tell me why you think I'm a bad coach. Maybe we'll talk right under all the football championship banners Loyola has won since I've been coaching here."

Coach Jones took off his ball cap, put it back on, paced back and forth, shook his head furiously, and then took yet another deep breath.

"Since none of you were able to recognize that Maurice was running circles around all of you at practice today and every other day this week, I'll tell you what. Instead of hitting the showers, why not give me some laps? Not Maurice. The rest of you."

At that, Coach DeAngelis spoke up. "Bob, wait. Maybe you need to cool down."

"Back off, Massimo."

Oh no, Maurice thought. *If Coach Jones does this to the team, they'll only hate me more.*

He put up his hand. "Coach!"

Coach Jones pointed to Maurice, still fuming. "Maurice, you've got something to say?"

Maurice took a moment to try and relax. And then he spoke. "Don't do this, Coach."

"What?"

"Don't do this. Give me a chance to prove myself some more. Give me some time."

"Listen to the kid, Bob," said Coach DeAngelis.

Bob Jones's smirk was replaced by a smile. His face went from beet red to its normal bright pink. "Of course, Maurice. You know what? You're right. Guys, consider this your lucky day. Hit the showers."

The players lined up, went through the school doors, and into the dressing room. Vijay looked over at Maurice and gave him a reassuring nod, but didn't want to break the quiet.

André, though, had no such problem.

"So, I hope you don't think that little act of yours is going to make you some kind of hero," he said to Maurice, but loud enough for everyone in the dressing room to hear. "It doesn't change the fact that you're the coach's little pet."

It was Vijay who stood up. "Look, Willis, all you do is talk and talk and talk. What's your deal?"

But, before André could answer, Maurice looked over at Vijay. "Sit down, Vijay," Maurice said. "This isn't your battle. This doesn't concern you."

"What?"

"Vijay. Sit. Down."

Vijay shook his head and slowly sat back down on the bench.

"Smart move," André sneered. "The last thing this team needs is our worst player and charity case sticking up for our oh-so-great starting running back."

André's words hung thick in the air. There were nods of agreement from many of the Loyola players. Vijay didn't respond. Neither did Maurice.

The team members cleaned themselves up in brooding

silence, exchanging only glances before departing from the dressing room.

Maurice and Vijay then walked out together, the last two players to leave; they split up at the bus stop, neither saying a word.

CHAPTER 5
IN THE SHADOW

Maurice got on the bus and rode to his stop, a block away from his apartment building.

He walked through the front door, and rode up the elevator. The elevator smelled like someone had recently barfed in it. He got to his floor and walked into his apartment. Maurice saw his mom, still wearing her royal blue hospital smock, sitting at the kitchen table, close to a black laptop, which was cracked open.

"*Bonjour*, Maurice," she said, offering a warm smile.

And then Maurice exploded. "I hate it, I hate it, I hate it! I hate the fact that I am Fabien's kid brother! Everyone on the team hates me! Why can't I ever be me? Why do I *always* have to be The Streak's kid brother?"

Then Maurice heard another voice. It came from the laptop.

"Well, hello to you too, squirt."

Maurice's mom raised her eyebrows. "I was just about to tell you to say hello to your brother before your outburst. Fabien's on Skype with me."

"It's okay, Mom," Fabien's voice came from the laptop again. "I get it. I really do. Let me talk to Maurice."

Their mother nodded. Maurice sat down in front of the laptop, his anger replaced with embarrassment.

"Sorry, Fab. I didn't mean . . ."

"Don't worry about it. What happened?"

"Coach Jones named me the starter."

"Awesome!" Fabien smiled and gave a thumbs-up to the camera.

"I thought it would be, but everyone just stared at me and no one said a word. It's like they blame me for being related to you. Your shadow is everywhere."

"Okay, wait a sec, little bro. Did you see the game against Penn State last Saturday?"

"Yeah. Of course I did. You know we don't miss your games on TV. You were good."

"That's a lie. How much did I play in that game?"

Maurice thought a moment. He tried to remember how many times his brother was on the field. "Maybe ten plays?"

"No, try *four* plays. That was it. I touched the ball twice. That's because, despite all my high-school records, I'm just a freshman here at Michigan. No one calls me The Streak. It's like being a Minor Niner all over again. Okay, it's not quite that bad." Fabien chuckled. "But when I got here, I knew I had to be the back-up."

"That's because Archie Anderson is the starter."

41

"Right."

Maurice visited a lot of football websites, so he had seen the name before. And almost all of the experts predicted that Archie Anderson would be the top pick in the next year's National Football League draft. Maurice had read all about him. Archie was born in Detroit, set every high-school rushing record imaginable, and didn't miss a beat once he got to the University of Michigan. This year, the websites called Anderson the top candidate for the Heisman Trophy, which went to the best collegiate player in the United States.

"So I'm kinda living in Archie's shadow right now," Fabien said. "And guess what? Before that, Archie lived in the shadow of Chris Traylor."

Maurice had watched Chris Traylor play on *Monday Night Football* the week before. Traylor had won the Super Bowl with the Pittsburgh Steelers the previous season.

Fabien continued. "And before that, Chris Traylor lived in the shadow of another great player. At Michigan, you walk down the halls of the athletic department, and you see the plaques and pictures of all the guys who've won championships here. The guys who went on to the NFL. Guys who are in the Hall of Fame. We ALL live in a shadow, here. When you come down to the stadium in a few weeks, take it all in. The history of the place. The names on the walls. The fact that more than 100,000 people will be in the stands, and they expect to see you win."

"Okay."

"You have to do what the coaches here tell me to do. Know that your opportunity will come, and then grab it.

Make it your own. My chance hasn't come yet. But you are getting one now. Don't worry about why you're the starter. Just go out and run like I know you can."

"It's not just that. The rest of the team is making Vijay's life hell. They keep telling him he only made the team because Coach Jones feels bad for him — about Ronny."

Fabien's deep sigh caused the Skype connection to crackle just a little bit. "Well, I guess Coach Jones feels a bit responsible. He and Ronny were pretty close. There was a time, when Ronny started missing practices, that Coach Jones used to go out of his way to make sure he could get Ronny back on track. He used to give Ronny rides home from practices. When Ronny got arrested that first time, Coach Jones called the cops and then vouched for Ronny in youth court. He knew that, as a city councilor, his letter of support would help a lot. So when what happened, well, *happened*, Coach took it really hard. I mean, don't you remember him at the funeral? He couldn't stand up straight, because he'd been drinking all day."

"I remember that he was babbling."

"Yeah, well, no one blamed him. Everyone just figured it was his own way of handling Ronny's murder."

Fabien and Maurice were both quiet for a few moments. Then for a few more. Fabien finally broke the silence.

"Well, I've got to be at study hall in about twenty minutes, and it's a good fifteen-minute walk from here," he said. "So bro, before I go, just remember that it's not supposed to come easy. You play the game, there's always going to be people judging you. Got it?"

"Yeah."

The screen went dark. Maurice sighed.

How does my brother make it seem so easy? Maurice wondered.

"Your brother's footsteps are awfully large," Mrs. Dumars said. "Deep down, he knows that. But don't blame him for his success. He should be an inspiration to you, not a burden."

Maurice nodded, got up, and walked to his bedroom. He closed the door behind him and sighed. He wondered if the talk with his brother was supposed to make him feel better. Because it didn't.

★★★

Vijay took a scoop of rice from the serving bowl and slapped it down onto his plate.

His father, sitting across from Vijay at the dinner table, smiled. "For someone who has not said a word since he came into the house, you certainly have a big appetite."

Vijay didn't answer. He plunged a fork into the rice and trucked a heaping pile into his mouth.

"Vijay, your father is trying to talk to you," his mother said.

Vijay chewed, swallowed, and then took a big gulp of water.

"I think I might want to quit football," he finally said.

"Huh? Why?" said his father.

"Well, it's been made pretty clear to me that I'm not very good."

"Wait. Bob Jones told you that you aren't very good?"

"No, Dad. Not Coach Jones. My teammates. Over and

over I hear how I'm some kind of sympathy case. They say the only reason I made the team is because Coach Jones feels sorry for me because of Ronny."

"And you'd quit because of that?" Vijay's father stared at his son.

"Why not?"

"Well, son, we all live with it, don't we? Ronny's death affected us all. There's no shame in feeling sad or having other people make allowances because you're mourning a family member."

"Wait. Dad. Are you saying I should just be okay with people feeling sorry for me?"

"No, what I am saying is that you shouldn't see it as a reflection on you. You just go out and play your game. And you should be honoured. During Ronny's troubles, playing football was one thing that gave him joy. I am sure, somewhere, he is proud you are also playing for Loyola."

"But —" Vijay set his fork next to his plate, as he realized he had lost his appetite. "I'm not mourning anymore. I've moved on. That's why I don't like dealing with this stuff with the team. And sometimes I get the nagging feeling that I've been chosen to re-live Ronny's life."

"No one asked you or pressured you to play football." Vijay's dad turned his gaze toward the ceiling. "Oh, Vijay. You'll always be in mourning. Even though you think you might not be, you are. You will understand it one day."

I'd better understand it one day, Vijay thought. *Because I don't understand it now.*

"Can I be excused?" Vijay asked.

"Yes." His dad nodded.

Vijay left the dining room and walked upstairs to his room. He closed the door behind him and opened his closet. Underneath a pile of clothes, he found an old cardboard shoebox. He opened the lid. Inside was a pile of newspaper clippings. Vijay did almost all of his reading on a tablet or his phone, but when it came to something he wanted to save, he found that having the actual printed format felt more, well, permanent than saving or bookmarking a file.

He found the clipping that had appeared in the newspaper two days after Ronny's death.

VICTIM KNOWN TO POLICE
By Jayson Marks, Staff Writer

Metro Police have identified the victim of Tuesday morning's shooting in a Weston parking lot.

Ramanan Panesar, 18, was pronounced dead on the scene after his body was discovered Tuesday in a parking lot near the Weston GO Station, close to the intersection of Weston Road and Lawrence Avenue. Witnesses say they were awoken by gunshots at approximately 2 a.m. Tuesday.

Metro Police spokesperson Candace Nagy-Mills said that Panesar was known to police. He was scheduled to appear in court next month to face charges of theft in relation to a break-in at an Etobicoke Home Hardware store.

"This appears to be an assassination-style incident," she said. "But police continue to explore all avenues. We continue to search for witnesses."

Nagy-Mills confirmed that the Gang Unit is aiding with the investigation.

Panesar had dropped out of Loyola Catholic High School last year. He had played football for the high school team, including two years on the junior squad under the eye of Bob Jones, a city councilor who is rumoured to be considering a run for the mayor's chair.

"'Ronny,' as we all knew him, was a great kid who made bad choices," said Jones. "Unfortunately, our community has too many Ronny stories. This has to stop."

Nagy-Mills said that evidence suggests Panesar's killer or killers were known to the victim.

"It looks like there was no attempt to flee or defend himself," she said. "This looks to be the result of a criminal transaction gone bad."

Panesar's family refutes that claim. In a written statement, Rishi Panesar, the victim's father, claims that his son had turned his back on crime.

"There was no way that our Ronny would be involved in any kind of criminal dealings. He had made some bad choices in the past, but worked hard to make himself a productive member of society."

Vijay put the article back in the box. Each time he looked at the article — and then put it away — he felt like he was burying Ronny all over again.

CHAPTER 6
RUNNING UP THE SCORE

When the quarterback handed the ball to Maurice, it was like everything was in slow motion. Maurice could see the hole opening up in the heart of the defensive line. He knew exactly where his next one, two, three, four steps had to be taken.

Then he exploded forward, a burst of energy as he pushed forward into the hole. He felt the hands of defenders swiping at his ankles, but his strides were too powerful. They couldn't trip him up.

Maurice burst through the defensive wall; he then made a quick left turn, so defenders couldn't chase him in a straight line. He cut back so he was running straight toward the opposition's end zone. With ten yards left to go, he slowed down slightly, knowing that there was no one who could catch him.

He strolled across the goal line and into the end zone.

He turned to see Coach Jones on the bench, jumping up and down.

"Oh yeah, yeah! Eat that!" the coach yelled. "Eat it! That's my boy, you hear? My boy!"

Maurice turned and handed the ball to the referee, and jogged toward the bench. Some of his teammates shook his hand. Others offered half-hearted applause.

"Dude, why don't you celebrate?" Vijay yelled as he hugged Maurice. "That's your third touchdown!"

"Because we're now up 34–0, and it's not cool to rub it in their faces," said Maurice. "You got to act like you've been to the end zone before, and you'll be there again. And I don't know if you've been looking around — but it's not like many of our teammates are exactly jumping for joy."

As Maurice got to the sideline and crossed over to where the benches were, he was met by his coach. Coach Jones raised up Maurice's right arm like his star player had just won a prize fight. A few members of the team cheered; but most stood in a circle around the spot where André Willis sat on the bench, staring forward.

"Good blocking on that play!" André yelled. "Great job, team! With blocking like that, any running back is going to be unstoppable!"

Maurice ran up the sideline so he could high-five his offensive-line players. "Yeah, that's right! Great job on the blocks!"

None of Maurice's teammates put up their hands to receive high-fives. There were a few half-hearted mumbles of "thanks" and "good job."

But if Coach Jones had noticed André or the cool reactions from some of the other Loyola players, he didn't show it.

"You are killing St. Sebastian singlehandedly!" Coach Jones yelled at Maurice. And then, even louder: "I guess that St. Sebastian must be the patron saint of LOSING? Am I right, boys?"

Maurice felt another arm on his shoulder. It was Coach DeAngelis, wearing a Loyola sweatshirt.

"Nice run," he whispered into Maurice's ear. "I think you've had a good day. You should sit down for now. I want to put André into the game. He needs to get some work in and, well, this is a blowout. Plus, no need to risk you getting hurt. We have more games to . . ."

"What?" Coach Jones interrupted the conversation. His hand was on DeAngelis's shoulder. He tried to pull the assistant coach away from Maurice. "No, no, no. He can't come out of the game yet! He could rack up 300 yards rushing on these guys! We're not simply happy to win a game — every win has to be a statement!"

Maurice watched as St. Sebastian's kick returner fumbled the ball. Loyola players converged on the loose pigskin. The referee signalled that Maurice's team had gotten the ball back.

"Get back out there," Coach Jones said to Maurice.

Maurice ran into the huddle. The quarterback read out a series of numbers, which was code for the play that was going to be run. Maurice knew it called for him to take the ball, run toward the right sideline, and then turn upfield.

The team broke the huddle and Maurice got in position

behind the quarterback. The ball was snapped, the quarterback passed the ball to Maurice, and the running back beat everyone to the sideline. He then turned upfield, dashed untouched for forty yards, and into the end zone for another score.

Maurice handed the ball to the referee.

"You're killing these poor guys," the ref said to him.

"I know. And I guess I gotta keep killing them."

Maurice looked up into the stands and spotted his mom. She was speaking to one of the many reporters who were in the stands as well, spread out amongst the Loyola students and parents.

He saw his mom shaking her head, and then pointing her finger in the reporter's face. She crossed her arms and looked away, making it clear to the reporter that she was done talking to him.

"Hey, Maurice!" he heard Coach Jones yell. Maurice looked away from his mom. "We got the ball back again! I think you could run, for like 400 yards all by yourself! Go out there and get me another touchdown!"

André rolled his eyes as Maurice walked past him on the sidelines.

"I wish I could take you out of the game right now," Coach DeAngelis whispered in Maurice's ear. "I know this isn't easy for you."

"For the love of the game, right, Coach?" Maurice replied, expressionless, as he slid his helmet back on his head.

After the game, a 55–0 win for Loyola, Maurice emerged from the change room in his shirt and tie. His mom was waiting outside.

"*Bon match*," she said giving her son, who was a foot taller than her, a hug. "It was a very good game. How many yards today?"

"I don't know, I lost count," said Maurice. "Coach Jones said it might have been 400, which would be crazy. I don't know if Fabien ever rushed for 400."

"That is wonderful!" Mrs. Dumars clapped her hands together. But she noticed that her son didn't smile when she hugged him. "Don't worry, I called Fabien during your game, he knows all about it. He has curfew tonight so he can't talk later. Maurice, you had a very good game, no? Why aren't you happy?"

"Because after a while, it didn't feel so good. We just ran it up on them. And the better I did out there, the more my own team resented me."

"But you looked great today," she said, her voice heavy with a French Creole accent. "I don't always understand this game, it is very difficult to learn, but I know that if you keep running and don't get knocked over, you are doing well. And if this André you tell me about wants to sulk, let him. Your grandmother used to say to me, 'some people like to wear unhappiness like a warm coat.' Think about that."

"*Oui, maman*," Maurice said, even though he wasn't too sure what to make of what his mom had just told him. "I saw you talking to one of the reporters in the stands."

"Bah!" His mom waved her hand back and forth. "I thought he wanted to talk about you! Or maybe about Fabien! But he finds me and starts asking me about Coach Jones this and Coach Jones that. He asks me what I think of him coaching the football team even though he's the new mayor. I say to him 'what about my son, he's the big story.' You know what he says to me? 'I don't really know much about football. I'm here to cover the mayor.' My word! I told him to get away from me! I don't want you to be a part of the mayor's football sideshow. I don't want my son to be a circus act because the mayor's coaching the team. I want to see the reporters and people at the games because they want to see the players. Not Bob Jones."

Later that night, Maurice and his mom sat together in their apartment and watched the night newscast.

The newscast was led by footage of Bob Jones, right hand raised in the air. He was surrounded by reporters.

"This morning, Mayor-Elect Bob Jones became Mayor Bob Jones," said the reporter. "He was sworn in and the ceremony certainly had its fair share of memorable moments."

On screen was an image of several Canadian Football League hall of famers, all wearing jerseys from their playing days. They held up signs that read JONES NATION. The reporter continued: "Among the CFL legends on hand was former Argonaut Quinn 'Quick' Rogers, one of the greatest wide receivers in league history. He's made Toronto his home for the last twenty years, and has been a big booster of the mayor, who is also a high-school football coach."

"Toronto just scored a touchdown when they elected this man," Rogers's gold teeth flashed as he smiled into the camera. "This is the man who is going to make this the greatest city in the world."

The reporter's voice returned, and she spoke over footage of a muscle-bound man with body-permed hair.

"Also on hand was Toronto native Chuck 'The Cabbagetown Crusher' Roma. The Crusher has held the heavyweight belt twice in his career. Of course, that depends if you believe wrestling is sport or theatre — or neither."

"Oh, babbbbyyyyyyyyyy!" the Crusher screamed into the mic. "Mayor Jones is in the houssssssseeeeee! Whoooooooooaaaaaaaaa!" He then jumped up and down and rushed over to Mayor Jones, putting the city's new head in a mock headlock.

Maurice looked over at his mom and smiled. "So, Mom, remember what you were saying earlier tonight? About how you were worried that Mayor Jones was going to turn our football team into a sideshow?"

His mother groaned.

★★★

Vijay and Maurice stood on the edge of Loyola's practice field. Some of their teammates were already gathered near the fifty-five-yard line, crouched over and doing their pre-practice stretches.

Vijay crossed the sideline and rushed to the middle of the field. Maurice put on his helmet and followed.

As they were doing their stretches, Coaches Jones and DeAngelis arrived on the field.

Coach Jones, wearing a Cabbagetown Crusher T-shirt, under his unzipped Loyola track jacket, blew his whistle. "Gentlemen! Please gather over here! Now!"

The boys all got up from their stretches and went to a spot near Jones and DeAngelis. Coach Jones put his palms out, a signal to his players that they should sit down.

"Thank you, boys," said Coach Jones. "I know that the first game of the season was awesome. But one game doesn't win a championship. Simply being good isn't good enough. Every game, from start to finish, we don't let up. Ever. That's my philosophy. That's all I've got to say right now. Let's get to work."

"But remember, boys, you need to pace yourselves, too," Coach DeAngelis broke in. "It's a long season and you don't want to get too beat up." Then, he looked directly at André. "And everyone will get an opportunity to play."

Coach Jones laughed. "Massimo, when did you become a hippie? The best players play. Back-ups sit. Want to get off the bench? Be better in practice! We go all out, all the time! And let's get this right! I want to wrap up practice a few minutes early, I have to attend a dinner tonight!"

The boys got up. Coach Jones barked out the names of the defensive line players and told them to come with him.

Meanwhile, Maurice and Vijay went to join the offensive unit.

"Did you notice that?" Maurice asked Vijay.

"Coach DeAngelis?"

"Yeah. He wasn't clapping, was he?"

"No," said Vijay. "And trust me, I've pissed him off enough in math class that I know the look. That's what he was doing when he was standing there. He just sorta squints and it looks like he's got a grin like some kinda super-villain."

"You mean like the look he's giving us right now?" Maurice saw that Coach DeAngelis was approaching.

"Mr. Dumars, Mr. Panesar," said Coach DeAngelis. "I didn't know that football practice had become a little chat session for you. So sorry to interrupt."

"Sorry, Coach," Vijay said. "We're ready to go."

"Good to hear, Mr. Panesar. Very good to hear. Now, please go join your teammates on the offence. That is, after you've given me twenty-five push-ups each. Mr. Panesar, judging by your recent results in math class, I'm not so sure you can count that high. You'd better follow Mr. Dumars's lead."

Coach DeAngelis stomped back to where the bright orange water coolers were set up next to the benches. He grabbed a paper cup and filled it. He took a deep, long drink. Then he scrunched up the paper cup and threw it as far as he could.

"Hey . . . Coach . . . that's littering . . ." Vijay said as he strained through a push-up.

"Shut . . . up . . ." Maurice panted. "We're . . . in . . . the doghouse . . . as it is . . ."

CHAPTER 7
THE COACH'S CHALLENGE

Vijay sat in his living room, trying to focus on TSN *Sports-Centre*. The Leafs had just broken a pre-season losing streak, and the TV analysts were going over the replays — and then going over them again.

But Vijay couldn't hear what the roundtable had to say about the beloved Leafs' brief respite from futility. Even though his dad was in the kitchen and Vijay sat in the living room, Mr. Panesar's voice drowned out the TV.

It's after eleven at night and Dad is on the phone, Vijay thought to himself. *I didn't know Dad had any friends who actually stayed up past eleven.*

"It is ridiculous!" Mr. Panesar yelled into the phone. "We worked so hard on the campaign, our candidate was the people's candidate, and we won by a landslide. He's our most popular mayor ever. Ever! And, every day, the paper takes another shot! Do they not know how many of their readers voted for Mayor Jones? Idiots!"

The tablet sat atop the coffee table, in between the couch on which Vijay sat and the television set. Five minutes earlier, Mr. Panesar had tossed the device on the table in disgust, and had stormed to the kitchen so he could begin calling some of his fellow Bob Jones campaign volunteers. But Vijay was happy that, by leaving, his dad had left the TV room free. So Vijay was able to switch over from the local news to the sports highlights without his dad's usual complaints about needing to follow the exploits of the new mayor.

"It is a disgrace!" Mr. Panesar's voice was even louder now. "You bet I am going to write a letter to the editor. We'll see if they print it!"

Vijay leaned forward and snatched up the tablet from its resting place. He hit the power button with his thumb, and the screen flashed to life at exactly the same spot his dad had been reading the digital edition of the paper, which had been updated just an hour before. It was the same story that had led off the eleven o'clock newscast.

MAYOR ASKED TO LEAVE CHAMBER DINNER: ORGANIZER
By Lesley Morrall, with Files From Mike Yuan and Chelsea Berg

Toronto Mayor Bob Jones left tonight's Chamber of Commerce dinner before he could make a scheduled speech.

Mr. Jones's press assistant, Chuck Mather, said

the mayor was ill and had to leave. Mather said the mayor's speech will be rescheduled, possibly for the Chamber's annual Christmas charity drive kick-off luncheon, which is scheduled for the end of the month.

But an organizer of the Chamber dinner said that the mayor was in fact asked to leave. He alleges that the mayor was "likely very inebriated." The organizer also said that Mayor Jones made "several inappropriate and lewd comments" to Chamber President Libby Grossman.

Mather called the allegations "unfounded and ridiculous."

"It seems that, in the eyes of his opponents, Mayor Jones is not even afforded the luxury of being sick," he said. "This week, the mayor has undertaken an exhausting schedule. He was sworn in, unveiled his new transit strategy and his plan to cut city expenses by 7 per cent. But the media continues to be more interested in tracking down imaginary scandals."

Mayor Jones did not return phone calls. Grossman chose not to comment.

An official from Polaris, the firm that handles security for the Boulevard Club, the posh venue that hosted the dinner, confirmed that his staff removed an "unruly patron" from the event. But, to protect the privacy of the individual involved, Polaris Chief of Operations Paul Burke would not reveal the identity of the patron in question.

"We referred the matter to Toronto Police," said Burke.

Toronto Police spokesperson Marc Beauchemin said no arrests were made at the Boulevard Club.

The mayor is already facing heavy criticism after skipping a meeting with the Gay and Lesbian Alliance in favour of coaching his high-school football team at Etobicoke's Loyola Catholic Secondary. The mayor pledged that he would meet with leaders of Toronto's LGBT community at a later date, but Gay and Lesbian Alliance Executive Director Beth Grieves said that, as of yesterday, the mayor's office has yet to return her calls.

On Thursday, Jones unveiled his ambitious $1.5 billion subway extension plan, even though the Ontario and federal governments have yet to pledge any funding to support such a project.

Vijay put down the tablet. His dad was no longer speaking in English; so Vijay knew that it was Uncle Rishi who was now on the line.

Vijay grabbed his smartphone from his pocket and started texting Maurice.

PRACTICE MIGHT SUCK TMRW.

His phone buzzed when Maurice responded.

AS IN, MORE THAN USUAL? LOL.

★★★

"Aw, c'mon! You, 72! You're killing me!"

"Hustle! Yeah, you. Slow and slower. That's all you got!"

"Look at you, over there, number 68! Yeah you! Don't think I don't see you sitting on your fat ass, doing nothing!"

Vijay was playing catch with Loyola's quarterback. But, time after time, he would take his eyes off the ball and yet another pass would hit the ground.

"Come on, man!" the quarterback groaned. "Do you ever want to get into a game this season? Start catching some balls!"

"Sorry, sorry," Vijay put up his hand. "It's just that I keep hearing Coach Jones screaming at the defensive players over on the other side of the field. It's kinda distracting."

André was hopping through a set of tires that had been laid on the ground. One hop, then into another tire, then hop out again. When he'd finished the circuit, he turned and looked at the quarterback.

"Vijay could drop a hundred balls and he'd never get cut."

Maurice jogged by. He wasn't wearing a helmet or pads. Coach Jones had made a new policy before practice began: that his newly anointed star player didn't have to do anything but have a light jog on the days before games.

"Glad Jones is yelling at the defence and not us," Maurice said.

"Well, I got plenty to deal with," Vijay huffed and puffed. "And André has decided he needs to comment on my performances as well."

"Well, you saw the news yesterday. You knew he was going to show up to practice awfully ticked."

"Yeah," said Vijay. "I saw it, all right. And I'm sure my dad's going to talk about conspiracy theory after conspiracy theory when I get home."

The quarterback tossed another pass. It went over Vijay's head. Maurice leapt and caught it.

"Hey, over there! On the offence! I may be over here coaching the defence, but I can see you guys slacking off!"

Vijay looked away from Coach Jones's direction.

Coach Jones marched forward and pointed to Vijay. "Number 81! VIJAY PANESAR! You! I see you just jerking around over there! Go and give me five laps! Now!"

Vijay dared not to say a word. He simply walked toward the sideline so he could do the laps.

"I can't believe this!" André howled. "Vijay is actually being called out for being so terrible. Maybe there is some justice, after all!"

"You're walking out there!" Coach Jones's growl carried across the practice field. "Panesar! You think you can lollygag your way around there? On second thought, give me ten laps! Or just keep running 'til we're done practice!" Coach Jones looked back toward his defensive team. "And, you, there, 68! Fat ass! Go join him out there! You're probably going to go home and eat two family-size bags of chips, so you may as well work it off ahead of time! And Willis! I heard your smart-ass comment! In fact, I hear your smart-ass comments all the time! C'mon, let's have some hard laps out of you, too!"

A whistle sounded. It came from Coach DeAngelis.

"Wait a second, guys!" Coach DeAngelis clapped his hands. He jogged over to Coach Jones.

"Bob, Bob. We can't ruin the kids with hard running the day before a game. We need them fresh." He tried to put his arm around Coach Jones.

But Coach Jones shoved DeAngelis away. "So, you're telling me that you want these kids to be lazy. And what would make you think any of those kids would be starting tomorrow?"

"Wow," Vijay heard the quarterback say under his breath. "I thought you were getting special treatment from the coach. Maybe I was wrong."

"Or maybe it's a different sort of *special* treatment," Vijay hissed back. "I think he let me make the team just so he can torture me."

Coach Jones cleared his throat loudly. All of the boys stopped what they were doing.

"You know, what Coach DeAngelis said about taking it easy on you guys has got me thinking. It has me thinking that we need to do the opposite. Each win has got to be a statement. Like tomorrow's game. Let's not just win, but send a message to every football team in Toronto! So, let's all do laps! Hard laps! Real running, not jogging. Except Maurice, of course; you just keep doing what you're doing, son."

A collective groan was heard from the players.

"Bob, that's nuts," said Coach DeAngelis. "These kids are playing tomorrow. We don't do that kind of fitness work in these kinda practices. We should be going over plays and walking through the playbook . . ."

Coach Jones put up his hand.

"Look, this is what they get, tough love. That's what they respond to. It's not just about football, it's about life lessons. They leave this practice field and they're in the jungle. They go back to their row houses and their single parents and tough apartment blocks. There's crack dealers on the streets and kids with knives in their socks. They come here off the boat and they need to fight to get out of here. They need to be tough as nails. If you want to keep taking it easy on the kids, you can go coach some team in some place where people have dogs with sweaters."

Vijay and Maurice looked at each other, mouths open.

"Take Vijay, for example," Jones kept going. "We've got to be tough on you. We all know your cousin died. Tragic, but it's a fact of life when it comes to this part of the city. Rexdale is a jungle. Weston is a jungle. Filled with monkeys ready to eat each other. Did you know that chimps murder each other, just like humans? Well, Vijay's cousin, I loved that kid like he was my son. But in the end, he was a gangbanger and he ended up dead. But Vijay knows he can't use that as a crutch. You can't have everyone feel sorry for you forever. You've got to move on. People live, people die."

What would my dad say if he heard this? Vijay thought. *He wouldn't believe it.*

Coach DeAngelis shook his head, and then blew his whistle. "Okay, guys, guess you got to do the laps." As the boys began to run, Coach Jones started to laugh. "And, guys, I have a bet for you! If you don't beat St. Leonard by twenty-one points tomorrow, well, let's say you don't want to be at practice on Monday!"

CHAPTER 8
A WIN THAT FEELS LIKE A LOSS

Maurice had been reading his tablet on the way to the game: The Tattler, a famous gossip website in Hollywood, had just posted a video of Bob Jones on its landing page.

Coach has become an international star. Crazy, Maurice thought as he clicked on the video as he rode on the bus.

The video — pixelated to the point where it looked like a video game from the 1980s — appeared to show the mayor standing in a restaurant.

Then came the voice-over.

"We just can't get enough of the crazy mayor from Toronto! And we thought all Canadians are so polite and mild-mannered. Not Bob Jones!"

Music started to play in the restaurant, and Bob Jones got up and started to dance. He shook his hips. He raised his hands in the air. And then he began to sing.

"Oh, no one is gonna stop Bob Jones, man," he sang

— or Maurice thought it was at least an attempt to sing.

He then spun. "Y'all try to stop me. But da peeps in my hood got my back. Da Jews in da press try to toss me out, try to crucify me . . ."

The video caught the sound of applause from other restaurant patrons.

Bob Jones picked up a bottle and took a long swig. Then he began to sing again. "Da media out to get me. Da faggots out to get me. Da leeches out to get me. But I'm just a guy from da hood, just representin' my peeps."

The voice-over continued: "We're not sure what's more racist: the anti-semitism or the put-on street accent. Or maybe it's the homophobia. But what's up with the people of Toronto? They elected this guy!"

Two hours later, and Maurice was on the field, a football cradled in his right arm. He didn't need to look down to see the yellow jersey of the St. Leonard Lions' linebacker; he simply felt the arms wrapping around his ankles.

But Maurice could hear Coach DeAngelis's voice in his head. *Don't stop moving your feet.*

Maurice kicked his right foot forward with all his might. He was either going to break the defender's hold or go sprawling face-first into the mud. He heard the defender cry out and the pressure on Maurice's legs was gone. Maurice put his left foot forward, then his right. The yard markers, reduced to runny white strips by the rain, passed under his feet more and more quickly. He saw another St. Leonard defender rushing at him. Maurice lowered his shoulder and extended his right arm. When the would-be tackler got close, Maurice simply shoved him away.

The path was now clear to the end zone. Maurice took three splashy steps into it, and turned to see the line judge extend both arms upward — the touchdown signal. Maurice looked back to make sure there were no penalty flags on the field. Satisfied that the touchdown would count, he walked over to the official and handed him the ball.

"Kid, it's okay to spike it," said the line judge.

"Act like you've been there before, and that you'll be there again," Maurice replied.

Vijay waited for Maurice on the sidelines with both hands extended for a double high-five. "Second touchdown today! Awesome!"

Maurice smiled. "If we get the extra point, we'll be up 28–7. That's the twenty-one-point margin the coach wants."

Vijay laughed nervously. "You're worried about that, too, huh?"

The point after went through the uprights.

Maurice draped a rain slicker over his shoulder and sat on the bench. Vijay sat next to him.

"So how much time is left? A minute?" Maurice asked.

"Yeah, fifty-eight seconds, actually."

"So, Vijay, St. Leonard still has time to score."

"Not much time, but it's possible. They scored on us way back in the first quarter, haven't got close to our end zone since then."

"Vijay, do you think that maybe Coach was joking?"

"He has to say stuff to scare us, to make sure we don't slack off. It's been a good day. But, even if we didn't win by twenty-one, well, what's the worst he could do? I mean, we're not pros — we're kids. He can't get away with torturing us or anything."

"You sound like you're trying to convince yourself," Maurice said.

"AW, C'MON!" the boys heard Coach Jones's voice boom across the sidelines. "Can't you cover a kickoff, boys?"

Maurice and Vijay saw that St. Leonard's kick returner had been allowed to bring the ball all the way back to the Loyola side of the field before he'd been brought down.

"Don't let up!" Coach Jones, who wore a T-shirt and shorts despite the fact that it was raining and only a few degrees above the freezing mark, yelled at the Loyola players coming off the field. He then picked one out of the crowd, marched up to him and grabbed him by the face mask.

"I saw you miss that tackle! We all saw it! You're useless! You need to decide if you're a winner or a loser!"

With just a few seconds left in the game, the St. Leonard quarterback lofted a pass toward the end zone. It bounced off a defender's hands and into the arms of a wide receiver. Touchdown. It wouldn't come anywhere close to keeping Loyola from winning but, after the point after was converted, the lead was shaved to 28-14.

"It's okay, boys," Coach DeAngelis walked up and down the sideline, clapping his hands. "We'll learn from this. That's why we need to take the big leads — in case we make mistakes. We still get the win, we'll be okay."

"Oh, we'll learn from this, all right!" Coach Jones stared at the Loyola players on the bench, and the defensive team that was coming off the field. "I will tell you now, boys, when practice comes next week, bring a bucket to the field with you! You'll need something to barf in!"

Coach DeAngelis looked back at Bob Jones, but didn't say anything.

"You better bring those buckets!" Coach Jones screamed. "And maybe a defibrillator for some of you fat-asses! Disgusting! You had it in you to kill these guys! Kill 'em! And that's what you leave behind?"

And then Coach Jones took a deep breath, which sounded like a wheeze.

"Okay, okay. I shouldn't have told you guys off like that, because there is still time left on the clock! Let's just play these last few seconds. We can still get that twenty-one-point margin. Maurice and the first team, you're back out there on offence. We've got about twenty seconds, we can run a couple of plays, as long as you guys get out of bounds and stop the clock."

André sat on the bench, shivering under a rain slicker. Vijay sat next to him.

"I can't believe I'm sitting next to you," André growled at Vijay. "But I guess this is the bench for the guys who never get in the games. Welcome to the big loser bench."

"Get over yourself," Vijay spat at him. "It's two games now that Maurice has totally shredded the other team. You can't pretend you're not noticing that. You can't tell me you're still holding onto this brother-of-The-Streak thing. Let it go."

André stared ahead, so he wouldn't make eye contact with Vijay. But his lips moved. "You'd better hope you continue to be on this team, that you're not kicked off. Because the second we're not teammates, I am going to kick your niner ass."

Vijay looked away from André and saw Maurice splish-splashing his way to the Loyola huddle.

"Wait a sec," one of the St. Leonard players yelled. "There's like no time on the clock, and you send your first team out there? You're not going to kill the clock and end the game?"

The quarterback threw a screen pass to Maurice. He ran twenty yards down the sidcline, but made sure to stay in bounds, so the clock wouldn't stop. He cut back into the middle of field and then threw himself to the ground. He was touched by a St. Leonard's tackler. There was no time for another play.

"Damn! Must have slipped!" Maurice yelled loud enough for the bench to hear.

As Maurice slowly rose to his feet, covered in mud, Coach Jones approached. He was on his way to the opposite sideline to shake the opposing coach's hand. As Maurice rose, Coach Jones paused to say a few words to his star running back.

"Look, it's too bad you slipped on that last play. I think you might have been able to go all the way. Too bad, I gotta keep my word. This is a win, but to me, it feels like a loss."

Then Coach Jones continued on his way to the other bench. The opposing coach refused to shake Jones's hand.

"I hope you set a better example as a mayor than you do as a coach," the St. Leonard's coach said to Bob Jones. In fact, St. Leonard's coach made sure to say it loud enough for everyone on or near the field to hear.

Jones laughed. "Whose team is undefeated, huh? Who is gonna play for a championship? I'm the best coach in the league. My record speaks for itself."

"At what cost?" the St. Leonard coach yelled back. "At what cost, Mr. Mayor?"

As Maurice got on the bus to head home from the game, he turned on his tablet — and when he looked at the front page of the city's largest newspaper's website, he realized that there was no way the coach would go back on his word and take it easy on the team at their next practice.

MAYOR'S FLACK QUITS
By Lesley Morrall

Toronto Mayor Bob Jones's office has confirmed that it has accepted the resignation of press assistant Chuck Mather.

"We'd like to thank Chuck for his work on our campaign and the transition to the mayor's office," read a statement that was signed by Mayor Bob Jones. "There will be no other comment made at this time."

Mather had met with the mayor this morning, and sources close to Bob Jones's office said that the press assistant wanted the mayor to curtail his drinking — and quit as the coach of the Loyola High School Football team.

The mayor reportedly asked for Mather's resignation.

The controversy, less than a week after the mayor was sworn in, follows hot on the heels of allegations that he was too drunk to give a speech to the Chamber of Commerce. Witnesses claim to have seen Jones forcibly removed from the Boulevard Club's premises last night.

The shock resignation could be a sign that Jones's team is secretly concerned about the mayor's conduct.

"Someone had to be a lamb to the slaughter," said Dr. Vincent Khan, a political science professor and civic issues expert at Ryerson University. "But when someone close to a leader leaves so soon after a major victory, it is a sign of major cracks in that leader's camp."

CHAPTER 9
THE PUNISHMENT PRACTICE

Maurice had been thinking about it all weekend and through to Monday.

He spent Saturday afternoon with his mom, watching the Michigan game on TV. The Wolverines were on the road, playing Northwestern University in the Chicago suburbs. There were a couple of shots of Fabien on the bench, and the commentators talked about how this Canadian kid might be a difference-maker in the years to come. But even though Michigan was up by four touchdowns in the fourth quarter, Fabien didn't see the field.

But Maurice had a hard time focusing on his brother's game. When he saw the images of the green football field, he could only fret over what Coach Jones might have in store for Monday's practice.

We didn't win by enough points, thought Maurice. *And the coach is in a lot of hot water. I hope he doesn't take it out on us. But I have a feeling he will.*

Maurice turned on the TV and tuned into his favourite late-night Saturday comedy show broadcast from New York. It began with the roundest member of the comedy troupe wearing a hoodie that had "HIGH SCHOOL FOOTBALL" on it.

"Yo, I'm da mayor of Ta-ranna," the comedian said, waving his hands in the air. "And I may be a rich white dude, but I feel for everyone in the community. You are all my brothers."

Another comedian walked onto the set. "What about gay people?" he said.

The audience guffawed. The comedian playing Bob Jones tried to suppress a smile. "Well, I mean MOST of you are my brothers."

Then another comedian walked onto the set. "What about Jewish people?"

"I said MOST," laughed the faux Bob Jones.

A female member of the troupe walked onto the stage. "What about women?"

"Look, you can't be my brother, because you're my sister."

"But not if you're gay," said the group.

"But not if you're a Jew," said the group.

Finally, a black member of the troupe walked onto the stage. In a totally deadpan voice, he said: "But I AM his brother. Because, as a white man of privilege, the mayor of Ta-ranna understands the socio-economic ramifications of race in the twenty-first century. From the other side, that is. But, the thing is, he UNDERSTANDS it."

The audience broke into laughter, and Maurice decided to switch off the television set. He didn't know how to feel about what he just saw. He didn't think it was funny, though.

That night, Maurice lay wide awake in bed, thinking about the newspaper article. He thought about the comedy show. He thought about what he'd done in Friday's game. Had he kept going, he could have scored the touchdown. Had he kept going, there would be no consequences on Monday.

Why did I decide to disobey the coach? He wondered as sleep refused to come.

He saw a few of his teammates at church on Sunday morning. Maurice didn't remember a word that was uttered in mass. Every time he saw one of his Loyola teammates either sitting, kneeling, or standing during the service, he wondered just how bad Coach Jones would take his anger out on them on Monday.

During Sunday dinner, his mother disturbed what had been a very quiet meal.

"Maurice, you've hardly said a word all weekend. What is wrong? Something I need to know about?"

Maurice shook his head. "No. Nothing I can't handle. Football stuff." And then Maurice dug into his stew again, finishing it without saying another word.

Monday came and Maurice's eyes were dry from a lack of sleep. He almost nodded off in Mr. Cangelosi's class. Only a series of nudges from Vijay kept Maurice from falling off his chair.

Just after the final bell sounded, Maurice and Vijay met in the hallway.

"What is wrong with you?" asked Vijay.

"Just thinking about what Coach Jones is going to do to us today."

"Well, you can't worry about it. What's gonna happen is gonna happen."

"But, Vijay." Maurice looked at the floor. "I could have scored the touchdown that gave us the lead we needed at the end."

"You slipped. We all saw it."

"I didn't really slip. It was like something snapped in my head. I just went down."

"Because you're mad at Coach Jones? You wanted to defy him?"

"I'm not sure. Or maybe it's, well, well . . ."

"What?"

"Well, I haven't felt like a part of this team yet. I play my heart out and no one gives a hoot. Everyone's mad at me just because of my brother . . ."

"Wait!" Vijay put his hand up. "Are you saying that you think you might have gone down on purpose, just so jerks like André would get punished today?"

"Yeah. Maybe."

"Wow!" Vijay smiled. "Dude, that's awesome! I mean, I'd run however many laps and do it gladly just to see André suffer!"

Maurice shook his head. "This was not the reaction I thought I'd get."

"Look, since we're on the topic of Coach Jones, I talked

to my dad," said Vijay. "I told him what Coach Jones said about Ronny and how hard he's coming down on us."

"And?"

"And what? He just said to take it easy on Coach Jones, now that's he's the mayor he's under a lot of pressure. And he said he doesn't believe a word of the race allegations. And my dad may have a point. Coach Jones's campaign team is filled with people from the south Asian community. Then he asked me to go fold some invitations for this Coach Jones campaign party."

The boys got to the change room; many of their teammates were already in there. André glared at Maurice. The players got ready and headed out to the field. Coach Jones was already standing on the browning grass. He was surrounded by the reporters.

"Okay, boys, you're all here." He clapped his hands. "I want you to gather around me for a picture. I was just telling the reporters here about the video that's been going around. You don't have to be a genius to see that it's not me in that video. It's some leech *pretending* to be me. My lawyer has now issued statement to the media that says, legally, there is no way to prove that it is me in that video. It looks like a blob, it's so blocky and blurry. I think it speaks to the nature of our media that you all assumed that it was me. I'm a celebrity. People impersonate celebrities, right? Now, look at this team. I picked this team. Me. You see black kids, brown kids, short kids, fat kids. Poor kids. Not-so-poor kids. If I was some kind of racist, would this be my team? No! THIS is the proof you need."

The cameras clicked. The kids huddled around Coach

Jones and smiled. Then, the coach put his hands up in the air. "Okay, now, I need to ask the reporters to leave. Even in the pros, some teams don't allow reporters into some of their practices. And these are minors I'm dealing with. So now that I've answered your questions, I will need to politely ask you to leave the premises."

The reporters grumbled.

"As the guardian of these high-school kids, I could legally force you to not film them. I've been nice so far," said the coach.

Slowly, the reporters and camera operators packed up their things and headed to the parking lot. Some were on their phones, talking to their editors.

Finally, the cars and vans began to stream out of the parking lot. When the last one disappeared down the street, Coach Jones walked across the field to the parking lot, and opened up the trunk of his car. He then walked back on the field.

"Gentlemen," Coach Jones said. "First off, thanks for doing that for me. As you can all understand, I have to defend myself against these allegations. But, at the same time, a promise is a promise. And I have to follow through. I did a bit of shopping before practice today. I found a good deal on these buckets you'll find in the trunk. Please go to my car. Grab a bucket. Hold onto it. Once you've got your bucket, you may begin running your laps."

"How many?" a player asked.

"How many?" Coach Jones smiled. "How many indeed. Well, I don't think of this as five laps or ten laps. Let's just say I want you to jog and sprint, sprint and jog, 'til you hurl into that bucket you're carrying. Once you've puked in your bucket, I might let you stop."

The boys were dead silent. Not one of them moved.

"Come on," said Coach Jones. "Let's get this started. This would have been so much easier if you hadn't given up that late touchdown."

Each player grabbed a bucket.

"You too, Maurice," said Jones. "I know you had another good game on Friday, but everyone on the team has to take the punishment."

When Coach Jones blew the whistle, they sprinted as fast as they could until they heard the whistle sound again. Then, they jogged. The whistle went again and they sprinted. Then jogged. Sprinted. Jogged.

"My legs feel like they are on fire!" Vijay cried. "So. Hard. To. Breathe."

Maurice saw Vijay drop to the ground. He looked around the field and noticed several other boys had also fallen to their knees or on their backs. A couple of his teammates were hunched over their buckets.

Then he heard another whistle. A higher note — it was Coach DeAngelis's whistle.

"All right, boys, sorry I'm late!" he heard Coach DeAngelis shout. "I had a couple of parent meetings to get to. But I'm here now and I see what's happening here. I'm quite sure that the point has been made. Take five. Get a drink."

"DO NOT DO THAT!" Coach Jones yelled. "You're either running or you're puking!"

DeAngelis glared at Jones. "Bob, what's gotten into you?

Look at them. You've proven your point."

Bob Jones's face went from pale to purple in the flash of an instant. He took three large steps and went face to face with Coach DeAngelis. "I know we've worked together for a long time. But I've about had it with you trying to defy the rules we've set. We said the boys would get punished for not winning by three touchdowns, and now they're getting punished."

"No, Bob, that's not what's happening. You're not punishing these boys — you're *torturing* these boys. This isn't about making them better players or better men or even a better team. This is about you showing them that you're the boss. You're the boss of this city now, isn't that enough?"

Coach Jones leaned forward and snatched the clipboard from DeAngelis.

"The school made me the head coach of this team. *Me.* They gave me the right to make all the football decisions. And I'm making one right now. Leave. You're done here."

"You can't do that!" Coach DeAngelis took the baseball cap off his head and hurled it to the ground.

"I just did."

"I'll go to the principal! The school board!"

"Go ahead," said Coach Jones. "Talk to the school board. Talk to whoever you want. I own this neighbourhood. I own the whole city, now. You know that! I'm letting you walk away. If I wanted, I could crush you."

"You haven't heard the last of this!"

"Oh, I think I have. And Massimo, before you go, don't forget your hat."

Coach Jones took a deep breath. His face went from

purple to red, then to pink. He turned to face his team; all of the players had stopped running to watch the verbal battle between their head coach and their now ex-assistant coach.

"Boys, I am sorry about that." Coach Jones smiled. "Sometimes you have to make tough decisions. Sometimes you have to pull the weeds. I am doing the same thing at City Hall right now. Having to figure out who is really helping, and who needs to go. I have to make tough decisions every day. And what you just saw was a tough decision."

Does this mean we don't have to do any more laps? Maurice wondered.

"Okay, now, what just happened doesn't mean that you guys get around the rest of punishment practice," said Jones. His smile disappeared.

'Punishment practice?' Is that a thing? Maurice thought.

"You can skip the rest of the laps," said Jones. "But what I want you guys to do is go over to that spot next to the field. Where the long grass is. Drop and roll to the far fence. Then roll back. Then roll all the way back to the fence. And stop."

The grassy spot next to the football field was a favourite spot for Canada geese to stop. There was a gentle slope to the fence. So, when it rained, the rainwater would flow down the slope — and the spot by the fence would become a series of large, deep puddles. The waterfowl flocked to these makeshift ponds. Canada geese are attracted to ponds near short grass; and once they've decided to colonize a spot, it's nearly impossible to get rid of them. And they often leave many foul souvenirs behind.

"There's geese turds all over there," Vijay hissed at Maurice.

"Yeah. Tell me something I don't know."

"GENTLEMEN!" Coach Jones yelled and blew his whistle. "I don't see you rolling! Now! Or would you rather we just did laps for the rest of the week?"

Maurice and Vijay trudged over to the grassy spot with the rest of their teammates. They dropped to the ground. Backs down. They turned their shoulders and began their rolls.

Maurice hit a clump of dirt — or, at least he hoped it was just a clump of dirt.

The boys closed their mouths when the workout began, but rolling around with football pads on was hard work. When an athlete works hard, he breathes through his mouth. And, sometimes, things can go in an open mouth.

"Aw, gross!" Maurice heard a teammate scream.

Maurice rolled, but imagined himself in Michigan blue and yellow. He imagined himself playing against Ohio State. He imagined himself going the length of the field against Notre Dame. He imagined himself scoring a winning touchdown against Michigan State. He did anything but try to think about the goose turds that lay in his path.

CHAPTER 10
THE VICTORY PARTY

"So Vijay, are you trying to tell me that Coach Jones made you roll through goose poop?" Mr. Panesar tugged on his bright blue JONES NATION shirt.

"Yes, he did."

Mr. Panesar smiled, and then the smile transformed into a deep, hearty laugh. "This really is a good joke you have worked up. I assume your friend Maurice is in on it too. Maybe the mayor, too? A lot of fun! But now, Vijay, I must go mingle!"

Vijay sighed as his dad walked away. He watched him greet people wearing various Bob Jones T-shirts. STOP THE WASTE. BOB KNOWS BEST. JONES NATION. One shirt read: PEOPLE > BIKES.

Vijay didn't understand why anyone would worry that bikes could be greater than people. That was the case anyway — until a couple of hours before the party. The story was on the front page of a Toronto news site. Vijay only clicked on it because there was a picture of someone riding a super cool fatbike that he wished he could afford.

STOP BIKE LANE EXPANSION: MAYOR
By Keenan Wells

Toronto Mayor Bob Jones looked to make good on one of his major campaign promises today. In council, he introduced a motion that would put a stop to bike-lane expansion in the city.

"The tyranny of the two-wheeler must come to an end," he said. "We are spending millions of taxpayers' dollars on lanes that are only being used by cyclists, rather than putting that money into shoring up the Gardiner Expressway or building a new subway line. We need to think about bringing the people in from the outlying areas and to stop making people feel bad for wanting to drive their cars."

If passed, a series of controversial bike lanes slated to be added to several downtown streets would be mothballed.

James Morse, who owns the Queen Street West cycle shop, Saddle Soars, says the move would send a poor message to those who want to use alternative forms of transportation.

"It's dangerous to ride downtown; cars don't respect cyclists and too many of us have been seriously injured or killed simply because we want to take an environmentally friendly ride. The city should be backing cyclists, not opposing us."

Mayor Jones said he would also kill a controversial city tax on car sales and surtaxes on drivers' licences.

On the other side of the room, Vijay saw his mom talking to someone who looked a lot like Bob Jones. If you only took a quick glance, you could be fooled. But on closer inspection, this man wasn't quite as chubby as the coach, and his face was a different shade of red.

Vijay went to the refreshment table and grabbed a can of Coke from an ice-filled bucket. He popped open the top, took a long sip, and surveyed the scene in front of him.

The community hall was packed. Members of Jones Nation were eating, dancing, and laughing. They slapped each other on the backs and, every couple of minutes, would chant "BOB JONES! BOB JONES!"

The only thing that was missing was Bob Jones himself.

Vijay watched as the man who sort of looked like Bob Jones walked up on the stage at the far end of the hall. He had a microphone in his hand.

"Ladies and gentlemen," he began. "I am sorry to tell you our mayor could not be here tonight. If you don't know me, my name is Nick Jones, and I was Bob's campaign manager. And, as you can tell, we're also related. We're cousins."

A big "awww" was heard from the crowd.

"But the mayor, well, he had an executive meeting go into tonight. They are talking about the bike-lane initiative.

Or, rather, *killing* the bike-lane initiative!"

The crowd cheered.

"To all of you, thank you for your hard work. I know Bob appreciates all you've done. And he's reminding all of you that not only is he going to stop the waste at City Hall, he'll get Loyola to the title game. Again!"

Cheers and screams erupted from the crowd. Vijay watched his dad leap into the air.

The campaign manager walked off the stage, as Jones Nation clapped rhythmically.

Vijay took a long drink and grabbed a handful of potato chips from a bowl. As he was stuffing them into his mouth, his dad rejoined him. But his dad had brought someone with him — a tall, wiry man who wore thick black glasses.

"Son, I want you to meet Jimmy Costa," said Mr. Panesar.

The wiry man thrust out his arm. Vijay shook the extended hand. It was warm and sweaty and gross.

"I'm Vijay," he forced a smile.

"Pleased to meet you," said the wiry man. "I'm the school trustee for this area. You play for Loyola. You're doing us all very proud."

Vijay snickered. "Sorry, sir, but I have yet to get on the field this season."

Jimmy Costa raised his hand. "No worries, young man. You will get your chance, and when you get your chance, you will do us proud. Sports and extracurricular activities can do wonders for a young man. Especially someone at risk."

"At risk?" Vijay raised an eyebrow.

"Well, you know, Ronny . . ." Mr. Panesar smiled sheepishly.

"I *know* about Ronny, dad. He was my cousin."

"Well," said Jimmy Costa. "Knowing how it might have affected your family, I am happy you have found something at school to dedicate yourself to. Something to focus on."

Vijay took a long, deep breath before replying.

"Sorry to be rude Mr. Costa," he finally said. "But I see where this is going. Look, football didn't save me from the street or gangs. I play because I like it and, well, I thought it might help me meet girls. Well, that part hasn't worked out. Girls aren't into jocks anymore. They're into nerds and goths and punks. That football-player-gets-the-girl thing? That's just from old TV shows and *Archie* comics."

"Vijay!" Mr. Panesar's eyes opened wide.

"No, Dad, let me finish. I am sorry, Mr. Costa, but my dad has probably led you to believe that I cry myself to sleep over Ronny's murder. No. My cousin was a drug dealer. Simple. He was killed in a parking lot while making a deal. I don't think there's any point in feeling sorry for him. He was stupid. He was either going to go to jail or get killed. He got killed. Maybe he did us all a favour, because we might have all had to go to visit him in jail, instead. And that would have wrecked a lot of weekend plans. We should all stop talking about it and forget about him."

"Wow," Jimmy Costa said after a moment. "But, still, Vijay, if you ever need anything . . ."

"What do I need? I'll tell you what I need."

Jimmy Costa smiled but shifted uncomfortably. "What?"

"Well, you're a trustee. Can you tell a school what to do?"

"Well, not quite." Costa adjusted his glasses. "All the trustees have to vote on school issues."

"Okay, okay. Well, I'd like you to vote on something."

"And that is?"

"Getting Bob Jones fired as our football coach."

Jimmy Costa tried to maintain eye contact with Vijay. He was also clearly trying not to laugh. But the air escaped out of his lips in a way that sounded like a gross belch.

"Oh, Vijay, you are a joker! Your father didn't tell me that! We are at a party for Bob Jones, and you want me to ask the trustees to fire our new mayor!"

Mr. Panesar wasn't laughing. He glared at Vijay.

But Vijay wasn't finished. "Well, you see, Mr. Costa, Coach Jones makes us barf at practice, he torments us all, and even made us roll through a field of goose crap."

Jimmy Costa doubled over. He gasped for breath. He reached into his pocket, pulled out a blue inhaler, and stuck it into his mouth and sucked back. The laugh turned to a cough, and then back to a laugh again.

"Good thing we're at a party," Mr. Panesar growled. "Otherwise this would be causing quite the scene."

But Vijay had already turned around to walk away. He plunged into the crash bar on the YMCA hall's back door. It swung open and Vijay stomped out into the cold night. There was a playground just on the other side of the parking lot. He made his way over and sat on one of the swings. He looked back toward to the hall to make sure no one had followed him out.

He then reached into his pocket and found his wallet. After opening it, he found a small picture of Ronny. He scrunched it up into a ball and threw it across the playground.

CHAPTER 11

SMARTPHONE SHOCK

EDITORIAL: TOUCHDOWNS OVER TRANSIT

Our mayor needs to ask himself, does he put a football team ahead of the third-largest city in North America? Or does he believe that the public who voted him in will have the patience to wait out the gridiron season?

Yesterday, he attended a meeting on the bike-lane plan. He once again uttered his opposition to the expansion of bike lanes. But the mayor didn't do his homework. During the meeting, it was clear he didn't know the bike-lane plan well; he didn't know the timelines or the total budget. All he did was say that was he was against it.

There were two previous meetings on the

lanes, which the mayor — as our elected leader — could have used to better educate himself on the lanes. In those meetings, the financial burden of subway expansion was also discussed. But the mayor wasn't at those meetings — because they conflicted with practice times for his beloved Loyola High School football team.

By flouting meetings so he can coach football, the mayor is ignoring those very taxpayers he vowed to protect in his election campaign.

The smell of spices and meat from the Jamaican patty place next door to Maurice's apartment building was overwhelming. It was a welcome break from the diesel exhaust fumes belched from the caravan of buses that roared down Dixon Road at rush hour. Maurice was tempted to go in and buy himself a patty, but he knew that his mom was making his favourite Haitian dish for supper — *griots*, pork with hot-pepper spice and sour orange glaze.

Maurice pushed through the entranceway and into the lobby; the smell of ammonia was overwhelming and carried a chemical sting that brought tears to his eyes. He entered the elevator and rode up to his floor.

Maurice walked into his apartment and saw his mom working in the kitchen, beads of sweat on her forehead. There was a crackling sound of meat in the frying pan.

"Hi!" She turned and smiled. "It's almost ready. The rice is almost done."

"Hey, Mom. Smells great." Maurice opened a kitchen drawer and collected some forks and knives. He set them on a small table just outside the kitchen. He then set out some plates.

"A couple more minutes and then we can eat," his mom said. "And then I've got to head out tonight. Night shift at the hospital."

"But you worked the early shift today," Maurice said. "You were gone when I left for school."

"I worked the early shift at the restaurant," she replied. "But I am working the evening shift at the hospital. They called me in because someone else was sick. One thing about hospitals — they always need to be cleaned. Never a shortage of work! And, I can use the hours. You know, Fabien's new school in Michigan gives him a scholarship for football, but we still need the extra cash so we can go and visit for that big game, right?"

His mom emerged from the kitchen with a bowl of rice in one hand, and in the other she held a bowl of pork that shimmered from the burnt-orange glaze.

She sat down, and they both took large helpings from the serving bowls, and laid them on their plates.

"So, how was school today?" his mom asked. "Did our mayor ask you to do anything crazy today?"

"No, practice was cancelled. He had some meeting at City Hall that was too important to miss."

"Well, that's a change," Maurice's mom sniffed.

"And because he fired Coach DeAngelis, there was no one around to run practice. Some of the guys got together and tossed the ball around."

"And you were able to join them?"

"Some of the guys are okay with me now, some of the

other Minor Niners on the team. A couple of the older guys are okay because I stood up to Coach Jones that one time. So there was someone there that I could toss the football around with. But most the other players, well, they don't talk to me."

His mom smiled. "So, Mr. Jones was actually busy being the mayor of our city today? Funny that your coach decided to be mayor for a day after the newspaper blasted him."

"Mom, do you like Coach Jones?"

"Life's too short to hate someone you don't really know. But Maurice, I think he's become a big distraction. And your games are like a circus. I think our mayor has bigger problems than football now — he should look after them."

"But we've won every game. And he always puts the team ahead of everything else he does. That sorta means something to the team, I guess."

"Is he putting football first because of you guys? Or is it to fuel that ego of his?"

"What do you mean, Mom?"

Maurice's mom folded her arms. "Look, when Fabien was coming up through high school, and people started to realize just how good he was, all of a sudden this person and that person were out there telling anyone who would listen about how they should get some of the credit for Fabien's success. There are some people out there who want to take a piece of your success and try to make it their own. I think the football team isn't about you or your teammates. It's about Bob Jones. He can force all those reporters out of their downtown offices and make them go to the edge of the city so they have to watch him coach football. He can jump up and down and tell everyone he's a winner."

"But if he wins, we win, too."

"Ask yourself this. Honestly. Don't you think if you had a different coach, that you'd still be winning all your games?"

Maurice thought about it. Didn't the coach bring the Loyola players together? Didn't he pick the team? Didn't he pick who played? Or would those all have been the same decisions Coach DeAngelis would have made had he been in charge? Or any other football coach?

★★★

The next day, Vijay walked into the dressing room to get ready for practice. Most of his teammates were already there, but Vijay was surprised to see that they weren't getting changed into their football gear. Instead, they were sitting on the benches in their dress shirts and grey slacks.

Coach Jones stood in the middle of the room. He pressed his phone to his cheek.

Maurice walked in right behind Vijay.

"Of course I'll do it! Week after next? Great!" Jones smiled as he continued his telephone conversation. "Sure, I'll make sure that my people will clear my schedule. But make sure you put me up in a nice hotel, the best you got in Hollywood. And if you're flying me out there, I'm going first class, right? Yes? Yes! Got it! Great! Yup, send the confirmation to the office."

Jones pulled the phone away from his face and slipped it into his pants pocket.

"Sit down, sit down," Coach Jones urged his team. "First off, I've got crazy good news! The *Late Night Show*, that talk show from Los Angeles, wants me on as a guest in couple of weeks! It's amazing how much the whole continent is paying attention to me, to this city!"

"Do you think he understands that they're just bringing him down to LA so they can make fun of him?" Vijay whispered to Maurice.

"Honestly, Vijay, I don't think he cares, or even notices," Maurice whispered back.

Bob Jones slapped his hands together. "Okay, boys, you don't have to change into your gear today. In fact, as I was just telling the guys when you got in, you're all going to get the day off of practice today."

"What's up, Coach?" the team's starting quarterback asked.

"I'll get to that in a sec. I know that you already got a day off yesterday because I had to be at City Hall. We'll just go really hard on Thursday to be ready for Friday's game. And now, I've got some announcements to make."

"Here it comes," whispered Maurice.

"Guys." Coach Jones's face was as pink as a pig. "You might have seen some stuff in the papers, the writers basically demanding that I should quit coaching you guys."

There were some nods in the room.

"Well, I wanted to tell you not to worry about that. When I was a city councilor, I thought that most of the reporters at City Hall were leeches. Now, as mayor, I *know* that they are leeches. They just want to stir things up. So, don't worry, I'm not going anywhere! I am going to bring the championship trophy to my office at City Hall, and I'm gonna show it to all those cockroaches! Maybe they'll polish it for me!"

Some of the players closest to the coach started clapping. Slowly, the rest of the team joined in. Vijay was sure that anyone who was left in the school could hear the applause even through the thick door of the boys' change room. Even Maurice clapped at the end, although he was looking at his feet.

"Now, now — I've got another announcement! A better one!"

The players went quiet again.

"I've been thinking. When we go to the championship game, we've got to look the part. I mean, look at us. The numbers are fading on our jerseys. There are rips in some of them. The paint is peeling off the helmets. You don't go to the prom in a dingy hand-me-down, do you?"

None of the players answered.

"Of course you don't! You dress up! You've got a date to impress! So, we're going to dress to impress. We're going to be getting new jerseys and helmets delivered next week. Best part? You don't have to do anything — no raffles or fundraising or having to go out hat in hand."

Now the players began to make noise again. Hoots and hollers echoed through the room.

Maurice put up his hand.

"Maurice," Coach Jones said as he high-fived the player who was closest to him. "You got a question?"

"Yeah, Coach, I do," Maurice asked. "If we don't have to raise money for these uniforms, who is paying for them?"

"Ha! I am glad you asked that! My supporters are paying for them! These people supported the campaign, and now they're giving money to help me and the team too! See, my supporters, they're showing that they want me to keep coaching! People around the city might look down at us; they say we come from a bad neighbourhood filled with immigrants. We'll show them! We'll show them that we have the best football program in the province!"

Maurice nodded and looked back down at his shoes. He waited for the cheering to quiet down. Some of the boys began to walk out.

"Hey, Maurice, want to join us? We're heading to Woodbine Mall," the team's back-up slotback asked him. "We're going to enjoy getting out early. Maybe catch a movie."

From across the room, André scowled at the slotback. The slotback just shrugged. "What, André? Maybe it's time to let it go."

André simply got up and left.

What's this? Maurice thought. *Some of my teammates are treating me, well, like a teammate?*

"Nah," Maurice shook his head. "Thanks, though." He then looked at Vijay. "You going with them?"

Vijay smiled. "No, man. Just going to catch the bus and get home. Be nice to get an early start on math. I think Coach . . . er, I mean Mr. DeAngelis, has been especially tough on us in class since he was tossed off the team."

Maurice got up. "I'll walk with you to the stop."

The pair left the dressing room and then strolled out of the school. After they got outside and into the bus shelter Maurice looked around to be sure there were none of their Loyola teammates nearby.

"Did you get that, Vijay?"

"Get what?" Vijay asked. "We're getting new uniforms. We didn't have to practice today. That's it, right?"

"No, did you listen to Coach Jones? *My* team. The voters are supporting *me. Me. Me. Me.* Now he's all proud that he's going to be on some big late-night talk show. He'll blow off a meeting here in the city so he can coach us, but I bet that he didn't even think about our team's schedule when that producer from LA called. It's pretty obvious, isn't it? Every day he keeps coaching us, the more this team becomes all about him. Heck, he's planning to take *his* trophy to *his* office at City Hall. What about us, Vijay? What about us?"

"Actually, I was more stunned by the fact that some of our teammates spoke to you — and it wasn't to insult you." Vijay felt his phone buzzing in his pocket. "Let me grab this."

Vijay put the phone to his ear. "Hi. What? Oh my. No! What! WHAT! No, really? NO! Where can I find that? What's the address again? Holy crap. I'm with Maurice. He's going to lose his MIND!"

Vijay disconnected the call and began to furiously type on his phone's screen.

"Oh man, Maurice, I gotta find this website! Now!"

"What's up?" Maurice asked, trying to peek at Vijay's phone.

"That was Maya from chem lab."

"The one that thinks you're cute?"

"Yeah, well, not important right now, Maurice. She said

it's all over the news. There's pictures of Coach Jones at a party."

"Okay, more of Coach Jones, just what I need in my life." Maurice rolled his eyes.

"No, get this — she says there's a story that's going all over, about the coach doing drugs at some party. The pics are all over the Internet. She said it's on this newshound.com site. Wait for it . . . here it is. 'Toronto mayor hits the pipe.'"

"Click on the link!" Maurice walked behind Vijay so he could look over his friend's shoulder.

"Here we go!" Vijay said. He and Maurice waited for the picture to load on the screen. The text appeared at the top of the page: "Toronto mayor hits the pipe; a scene from a wild party."

"Man, how slow is this loading?" Maurice said.

"The site must be overwhelmed," Vijay laughed.

They waited. And waited. The screen was blank for five seconds. Ten seconds. And then, slowly, the picture appeared — as if it was coming through an old-school dial-up connection. But, as soon as he could take in most of the photograph, the smile disappeared from Vijay's face. He dropped the phone, turned, and ran away from the bus stop as fast as his legs could carry him. He ran past the plaza where he and Maurice liked to go for burgers. He ran until he found himself in a small park. And then he collapsed onto the ground, gasping for air.

Back at the bus stop, Maurice picked up the phone Vijay had dropped. He looked at the picture and his eyes went wide. He understood why Vijay might not be wanting his phone back anytime soon.

CHAPTER 12
A DOSE OF REALITY

Maurice wasn't surprised to see the signs on the wall the next day: FOOTBALL PRACTICE CANCELLED. FRIDAY'S GAME vs. POPE JOHN PAUL II HAS BEEN POSTPONED.

When Mr. Cangelosi called out Vijay's name in class and didn't get a reply, the teacher mumbled, "Of course, Mr. Panesar wouldn't be coming in today."

Mr. Cangelosi turned to Maurice. "I know this is an awkward question, Mr. Dumars, but do you have any idea when we might be expecting Mr. Panesar to return to school?"

Maurice shook his head.

"Understood." Mr. Cangelosi used a soothing tone of voice that Maurice hadn't heard from his teacher before. "I'm sure that this has all been very difficult for him."

Maurice tried to concentrate in class, but he kept

thinking back to the night before. After putting Vijay's phone in his bag, Maurice had spent an hour searching for his friend. He finally found Vijay in an empty park, sitting under a tree. Vijay was shaking, as if he'd been out in freezing temperatures for hours. But Maurice knew that Vijay wasn't cold. It was shock. After all, Maurice understood that nothing could have prepared his friend for what he had seen in that picture. Maurice wondered if Maya knew about what had happened to the Panesars — or else, why on Earth would she call Vijay and tell him to check out that news story and the photo?

Maurice asked Vijay if he wanted to catch the bus.

Vijay just shook his head. He mumbled something under his breath that Maurice thought was about not wanting to be around people.

"Then I'll walk you home," Maurice offered.

After forty-five minutes of walking through neighbourhood after neighbourhood, Maurice and Vijay came to the Panesar home. Maurice knocked at the front door, and Mr. Panesar opened it up.

"Thank you, Maurice," he said. "Is my son okay?"

"I think so. I mean, well, I don't know what to say. I mean, we all knew Ronny . . ."

Mr. Panesar put his hand on Maurice's shoulder. "I remember you and Fabien and your mom coming to the funeral. You have been such a good friend to my son, even through the death of his cousin."

"Thanks."

Vijay walked into his house silently. And, then, finally, he spoke. His voice was soft. But firm. "So, what do you think of Bob Jones, now, Dad? Feel kinda stupid, huh? Seeing that picture of him standing there, with Ronny handing him a bag of white rocks? I wonder what that could be, huh? And what was that in Bob Jones's hand? A crack pipe? Both of them smiling? How about that, huh? You know, when Ronny got into trouble, he was up for selling weed; now it looks like he was into a lot more. And Bob Jones was right there with him!"

Mr. Panesar nodded. "It is hard to explain. Yes. But, maybe we need to wait for Mr. Jones to speak. Already on the news, they say there will be a press conference tomorrow. We must try to be fair."

Tears began to stream down Vijay's face.

"The only reason you want to be fair is because you had, like, a dozen signs on the lawn! Because every T-shirt you own is a Bob Jones shirt. How does it feel, Dad? How does it *feel*? For a year, nothing I did in this family mattered. I work my tail off at school. I do everything you ask. I've never been in trouble. Ronny gets gunned down in a drug deal gone bad, and there's a shrine to him in our house! And then there's this Bob Jones obsession. Why? Because of Ronny! Did you think he'd bring Ronny back? And, well, how about me? Ever since Ronny died, the only time I exist is when I talk about Ronny!"

Mr. Panesar was silent.

Maurice backed away through the door and closed it behind him.

★★★

EDITORIAL: JONES MUST STEP ASIDE

Innocent or guilty, the mayor must step aside while authorities investigate the events that led up to this photo. But if he stays on board, the time we should be spending discussing Toronto's future will instead be spent on speculation about Bob Jones's private life. And in that scenario, everybody loses.

It is not for the editorial board of this newspaper to say whether or not the mayor of Canada's largest city and most important economic centre is innocent or guilty. The photo, while incriminating, has no context. We will be looking for answers in the days to come. It is up to the mayor to provide them. And, to ensure the best outcome, the mayor cannot be trying to run a city while, at the same time, having to answer to these very serious allegations.

Maurice closed his locker door. Mr. Cangelosi's first-period class was over, and he had about five minutes to get to his next class — if it had been a normal day. But it definitely wasn't a normal day. He knew he wasn't likely going to make it to his second class on time.

Maurice heard the chatter in the hallways.

"Are you gonna watch it?"

"Let's all watch it!"

"The press conference is at ten. It's going to be streamed by all the local stations."

"Yeah, everyone in the school is going to be watching this thing. Heck, everyone in Toronto is going to be watching!"

"Did you hear the principal in morning announcements? I can't believe it— they really can't fire Coach Jones?"

"Something about how the school board has to decide; it's up to them. And about how we have to believe the coach is innocent because a photo doesn't prove he's guilty."

"That's messed up. We all saw the picture. He had a crack pipe."

"Do you know how many people are talking about the school? Check Twitter, we're, like, the most famous high school in the world right now!"

"I bet we're actually going to talk about it in my social studies class."

"Wasn't that Vijay's brother in the photo? That was in the news, wasn't it?"

Maurice stopped next to the person who had identified Ronny in the incriminating photo.

"Cousin," Maurice said in a measured voice. "But he was like a brother to him. A long time ago."

But Maurice's worries were much smaller. He wondered if the football season would be put on hold.

There were already groups of kids throughout the hallway huddled around the people who had the best smartphones or tablets with nice bright displays. They were all waiting for the Bob Jones press conference to begin.

Maurice found a spot where a group of students sat or crouched in a semicircle around an iPad that was perched against a wall. The tablet's screen went from blue to a shot of a podium that had the City of Toronto logo on it. The shot pulled back; there were cameramen and reporters and microphones surrounding the podium. In the corner of the screen were the words: "LIVE. CITY HALL. TORONTO."

A man walked up to the microphone. He looked like Coach Jones, but he wasn't Coach Jones.

"Hello," said the man. "I am Nick Jones. For those of you who aren't usually on the City Hall beat, I am Bob Jones's cousin. I helped out with the campaign. Nice to meet all of you reporters I haven't seen before. As for the ones I do know, well, hello."

Nick Jones took a deep breath. He pulled a folded white piece of paper from his suit pocket. After slowly unfolding it and placing it on the podium, he began to read. As he spoke, he did not look up at the cameras or the reporters around him. "I have known Bob since we were kids. We went to the same high school — go Loyola! Knowing Bob as well as I do, spending as much time with him as I do, well, I find the allegations in the media to be shocking. But, the mayor will be out in a minute to make a statement. And that will be all. And I want to make this clear: The mayor will not be taking questions about this topic. He will say what needs to be said and we will close the proceedings for the day."

Then Coach Jones walked to the podium, as his cousin stepped aside. On the broadcast, Maurice and the other kids huddled around the phone could hear the clicks of cameras and the cries coming from the reporters.

"Ladies and gentlemen. As my cousin — and one of my biggest supporters — has said, I will be making a statement. I have been advised by my legal team that I should not be answering any questions. I don't want anyone to think that means I have something to hide. I don't. But I have to respect the wishes of my lawyers. But I also want to be honest with the public and the great people of Toronto who supported me and our campaign to end the waste at City Hall."

He's going to quit, thought Maurice.

Maurice remembered going to Loyola games back when Fabien was a Minor Niner. Fabien was running over tacklers like they weren't there. But then Maurice remembered how Coach Jones would yell at Fabien on the sidelines. Jones said that good wasn't good enough, that Fabien had the tools to be the best. Jones warned Fabien that, even though it seemed easy, he had to work harder. He told Fabien that, with football, he could repay his mom for all the hours she put in at work, making sure there was food on the table.

What happened to him? Maurice wondered. *Or was he always this self-centred, this crazy, and we just didn't see it?*

The mayor cleared his throat, and then looked straight ahead.

"As many of you have seen, the newspapers and several websites have run pictures of me with what looks like a, *ahem*, crack pipe in my hand. And, today, these reporters, the same people who harass me when I coach my football team, who have been trying to get rid of me since I got elected, well, no surprise that they jump to conclusions and say that I am a drug abuser.

"Nothing could be further from the truth. Yes, I was at a party. Were there drugs being used there? Likely. This picture was taken back when I was a city councilor, and represented a neighbourhood that has many people who deal with drug issues. Should I pretend they don't exist?

"In fact, the kid in the picture next to me, Ramanan Panesar, he was a kid I knew from the neighbourhood I represented. As you know, he died tragically last year. Nothing will make me happier than knowing that day when his killer or killers have been brought to justice. I know his family — and they supported me in the election campaign. And to them, and to the rest of the city, I say this. I do not smoke crack. The pipe in my hand, well there is an explanation there, but I have been advised not to discuss this because the leeches in the press will take what I say and then turn it into something else."

"Will you resign or step aside?" a reporter called out.

The mayor continued with his speech, ignoring the question.

"I welcome an independent investigation because I am sure it will clear me of any wrongdoing. Once and for all, we need to expose the leeches in this city, the people who want us to fail, who want Jones Nation to fail. I am an innocent man, and I want to save your tax dollars. I want to bring law and order to this city so we don't have more cases like Ramanan Panesar. And to do these things, I need to be mayor. So, no, I will not step down. From anything. Not from the mayor's chair. Not from the people who supported me, like the Panesar family. And not from my football team, either."

The mayor stepped down from the podium and then quickly turned his back to the media so he could walk away from the throng as quickly as he could. But, before he could leave, the reporters flew up from their seats and surrounded him.

"Mr. Mayor, do you not feel this will be an unwanted distraction for the city?"

"Are you addicted to drugs?"

The mayor pushed through. "No more questions. I have said what needs to be said. Now, I am going back to my office because I have a city to run."

Maurice had been so engrossed in what the mayor had to say that he hadn't noticed that André was sitting next to him. Now that the mayor was no longer on the screen, Maurice realized that he was shoulder-to-shoulder with his nemesis.

"Rough," said André.

"Yeah," Maurice said, as he scratched his ear. Maurice always scratched his ear when he was in an uncomfortable situation. Sometimes, when he was in confession, he would tug at his ear so hard that it felt like he might just pull it right off of his head.

"Thing is, if the coach, I mean, mayor quits, our team might be finished," said André.

"Maybe."

"Look, don't think this means I'm okay with you stealing my starting job, but I don't know what I'd do without football. If we lost the team, well I'd need to find some other reason to actually want to come to school."

"If something happened to Coach Jones, I'm sure they'd find a way to keep our team going."

"I'm not sure," André said. "If there is no team, I won't get the chance to win my job back from you. And that would suck so majorly bad. I wouldn't be able to deal with that."

CHAPTER 13

VIJAY'S SURPRISE VISIT

On the way home, Maurice did something he rarely did: listen to talk radio. But he knew that the on-air person-alities would all be talking about the press conference. So, instead of listening to his favourite Drake mix on the way home, he was listening to Toronto's king of afternoon talk radio.

"This is Marv Mortensen, sitting with Shelly West, the chair of the Catholic School Board. So what you're telling me is that Bob Jones hasn't been removed? Suspended?"

There was a pause that seemed to last several seconds to Maurice. Then West finally began to speak: "We will have an upcoming vote on a possible suspension. We cannot ignore Mayor Jones's years of exceptional volunteer work with our Loyola team. We are troubled by the photos and allegations but, I must make this clear, Mayor Jones is a volunteer and not an employee. He is a volunteer who has cleared all the compulsory security clearances we expect for anyone working with minors. So, this is not a question of firing a staff member; it is a question of barring a citizen from school property, a citizen who has yet to be charged with a criminal act."

"Ms. West, you sound like a lawyer. Torontonians want action!"

"And yet your station is still broadcasting the mayor's weekly one-hour call-in show. And that's likely because you are dealing with some of the same ethical and legal questions. We will continue to monitor the situation. We will ensure that no student is put in harm's way."

"Thank you, Ms. West. But, before I throw over to the news, I should remind all our listeners that the boy in that incriminating photo with the mayor isn't with us any-more. Who kept *him* out of harm's way?"

Maurice opened the door to the apartment and was surprised to find Vijay sitting at the kitchen table.

"Look who decided to come over," Maurice's mom said. "It's been a while since Vijay stopped by."

Maurice dropped his bag and walked to the table to sit. "What's up?"

"I wanted to talk to you. In private," Vijay said, wring-ing his hands. His eyes were bloodshot and there were dark circles under them. Vijay normally took pride in hav-ing his jet-black hair just right, but it was matted down at the top and scattered at the sides.

"Well, my mom is here, so it's not totally private."

"Yeah, well, I get the feeling your mom might be on my side. So it's okay."

Maurice's mom nodded in agreement. "Our friend here feels like he's got no place to go."

Vijay sighed. "I couldn't go to school today. I just didn't feel like I could deal with it. My parents were home; my dad took another day off so he could watch the press conference. So, I sit there and watch it with him. And it's, like, super-stressful because we had that blow-up last night. But at least, to make it worthwhile, I think, yeah, Coach Jones is going to quit. But no, Jones says that he's not only go to stay the mayor, he's not leaving the football team."

Maurice held up his hand. "But what did your dad say?"

"This is the best part, Maurice. *Nothing*! My dad, I swear he'd walk off a bridge for Bob Jones. As soon as Coach Jones talked about how our family supported his campaign, my dad started saying that, get this, he *believed* the mayor! He said we should all try to understand that there has to be an explanation. It was like he was all proud that the family name got mentioned on TV. I just had to get out of the house. Maurice, I have a father who worships the memory of my cousin. And now, he's worshipping the mayor. Problem is, there's no room for me in that temple he's built."

Vijay clenched and unclenched his fists and then kept talking. "What if he doesn't get charged? Everything goes his way. He tortures us at practice and no one says anything. And now we have proof that he was at a party with *drugs* and Ronny, and still nothing. I bet that the cops don't do anything. No one wants to be the one who gets in the mayor's way."

"I don't know what to say, man," Maurice said.

"I do," said Maurice's mom, steam rising from the mug of coffee in her hand. "Look, Vijay, I can't imagine how hard it has been for your family. I remember back when you all were kids. I'd drop Maurice off at your house and you and Ronny were waiting for him. Ronny was like your older brother. You can't blame your dad or anyone else in your family for trying to remember the best things about him. And they'll do their best to reject anything that suggests Ronny wasn't a saint. So, when this thing with Mayor Jones comes up, they want to believe everything the mayor tells them, because it keeps the memory of Ronny as a nice boy intact."

"Mrs. Dumars, can you talk to my parents and tell them that?" Vijay asked.

Maurice's mom shook her head. "They wouldn't listen to me, either." She put her coffee mug down on the countertop and clasped her hands together, as if in prayer.

"We've got to get Bob Jones out of Loyola," said Vijay.

Maurice rolled his eyes. "And how do you expect to do that? Vijay, if you haven't noticed, Coach Jones is still the most popular man in this city. On the way home, I saw a story on my phone, a poll was taken after the press conference, and they said the mayor still has a lot of support."

Vijay sighed. "Then we'll need to get help."

"Who would help us?"

Vijay sighed and stared blankly out the window as if one of the flashing lights from the airport in the distance would give him inspiration. "I don't know, Maurice. I just don't know."

★★★

After a week away, Vijay returned to Loyola football practices.

When he saw Vijay suiting up, André did something he rarely did. He spoke to Maurice — that is, he spoke to Maurice in a way that wasn't insulting.

"I can't believe that Vijay's here. He's either crazy or doesn't care. Maybe he's more hardcore than I've ever given him credit for."

"Vijay is tough. You've been too busy hating him to see it," Maurice said.

Vijay ran his routes. He caught the football. But not a word.

He came back the next day. And the day after that. In silence.

On the day before Loyola's next game, against Our Lady of Fatima, Coach Jones told Vijay that he wanted a private meeting after practice. Just the two of them.

After Vijay got changed, he walked to the school's athletic office. Coach Jones was crammed behind a desk. The office was tiny, and the wide body of Coach Jones looked like a Mack truck parked in a small-vehicles-only spot.

"Come in, Vijay," said Coach Jones. "We should talk."

"Sure." Vijay entered and sat on a stool near the entrance.

"Look, I just wanted to clear the air."

"Sure," Vijay said again. He was pretty certain that, no matter what the coach said, his only answer was going to be *sure*.

"I know what you saw in the newspapers, what we all saw," said the coach. "I can see how tense you've been. And I've been instructed by lawyers to not speak about this

Ronny incident with anyone. The school board is going to prepare a report on me. But I decided I needed to talk to you one-on-one."

Coach Jones paused, clearly waiting for Vijay to say something. After a few seconds of very awkward silence, the coach apparently decided the best course of action was to continue.

"Vijay, you deserve a straight explanation. I was at a party with your cousin. Yes, there were drugs there. But, really, I was trying to help people. You can't help people without going to them. It broke my heart that Ronny was into drugs and was hanging out with bad kids. Your family has always been close to me, from the time I was a councilor from this ward who sat in the back corner of the council chamber, you get that?"

"Sure."

Bob Jones extended his arms from behind the desk, as if he wanted Vijay to come over for a bear hug. Vijay didn't move off his stool. "It's okay. Really. You've been through a lot. I just wanted you to know I am on your side, that I'm always on your side. And the people who are on my side? I treat them right. I look after them. You understand that, Vijay?"

"Sure."

"That's great!" Coach Jones brought his hands together. "So, we're going to get 'em in the next game! I'll look after you, you see?"

CHAPTER 14
VIJAY'S CHANCE

MAYOR ACCUSED OF REDIRECTING CAMPAIGN FUNDS TO FOOTBALL TEAM

TORONTO (CP) — A former staffer of Toronto Mayor Bob Jones is blowing the whistle.

Chuck Mather, who was the mayor's media flack throughout the election campaign and the first few days of the mayor's term, says that the embattled Jones must come clean about directing office expenses and budgets toward personal pet projects.

Mather resigned his post after Jones was escorted from the posh Boulevard Club, where he was supposed to give a speech. The resignation came just days after Jones was sworn in — and rumours have swirled about the reasons why Mather left so abruptly.

But, this morning, Mather made it clear he isn't going to protect his former employer.

"The day that he was sworn in, the day that he moved into the new office, he called a meeting and said we had to find a way to direct some of the surplus funds raised through the election campaign to help buy his high-school football team new uniforms. I reminded him that it was not city policy for staff to spend working hours on non-City of Toronto business."

What Mather is saying was that it wasn't just about the alleged re-direction of funds, but that the mayor's staff were expected to spend working hours — which come out of the taxpayers' pockets — on finding a way to shift the money to the football team.

City Councilor Harjit Singh says he was not surprised to hear of Mather's allegations.

"There were rumours about this in City Hall even as Mayor Jones was being sworn in," he said. "Now we have a smoking gun."

The mayor's office issued this statement: "Mayor Jones will not comment on these baseless allegations. He is proud to have helped raise funds for the Loyola football program, and believes it has not impacted the mayor's office in any way."

The next night, Vijay's name was in the starting lineup. He hadn't played a down all season, and he was suddenly thrust into the limelight.

When he saw the lineup sheet, Maurice whistled. "Wow, look at that. Good for you, Vijay."

André walked past the team sheet and rolled his eyes.

"I don't think I'm on the list because I've been playing well in practice or anything," Vijay whispered to Maurice.

"Well, you're playing," Maurice said. "Go out and make something happen."

"It's funny," Vijay said. "I know the coach is starting me for all the wrong reasons, but I kinda wish my dad could be at the game so he could see me play. He used to come with my uncle all the time when Ronny played."

But there was no way Mr. Panesar would be at the game. He had texted Vijay in the middle of the day about how angry he was about the latest Bob Jones exposé.

For the first drive of the game, Coach Jones didn't call running plays. Instead, the quarterback threw the ball to Vijay on three separate occasions. The next time Loyola got the ball, four more passing plays were called, all with Vijay as the primary receiver. Loyola's success had been built on Maurice's runs, but on this Friday evening — even with a decent breeze making the passing game difficult to execute — the coach kept calling for Vijay to get the ball.

Vijay took a short pass, shook off a defender and scampered into the end zone. But, on the next drive, after making a catch, he was hit from behind and the ball came loose. The fumbled ball tumbled in the dirt before being pounced upon by a Fatima linebacker.

Vijay tiptoed to the bench, expecting to receive a blast of anger from Coach Jones. Instead, Coach Jones hugged him. "It's okay, kid. Go get 'em next time!"

At halftime, Loyola was only up by a single touchdown, against a team that had yet to win a game that season. Maurice had only run the ball a couple of times.

"We just need to show that we can win without Maurice," Coach Jones said at halftime. "We have to show the other teams that we have other weapons on this team."

Then Coach Jones winked. "I've been nice to Maurice because I know he's got a busy weekend ahead of him. When are you leaving?"

"There's an overnight bus that leaves at midnight," Maurice replied. "My mom and I should be in Ann Arbor in plenty of time for my brother's game tomorrow."

"Well, you'll need to be able to sleep on that bus so you can be well rested for Saturday's big Michigan game." Coach Jones smiled. "We'll work you pretty hard in the second half so you can be good and tired for that bus ride."

True to his word, Coach Jones went back to Maurice in the second half. The big running back got the ball time after time, and by the end of the game, he'd scored three touchdowns and Loyola had won by twenty-eight points.

At no point did André rise from his spot on the bench and cheer. But he did say something in Vijay's ear.

"So, now you've started a game this season, and I haven't. I'm not so sure I shouldn't just go and kill myself."

This isn't about you, Vijay thought when he heard the cutting remark. He turned to André. He got awfully close.

"So, what am I supposed to do, then?" Vijay said under

his breath. "Did you ever think that I might be in a no-win situation here? I play, and you guys all think coach is playing favourites. I don't play, and you all think I'm a coward."

André didn't reply, save to sneer at Vijay before turning his eyes back to the field.

A cadre of reporters was waiting for Jones as the team walked from the sidelines toward the dressing room. The media formed a scrum about halfway between the field and the school's doors.

"Let's not go into the room yet," Vijay murmured to Maurice. "I want to see what Bob Jones has to say."

They tried to stand as far away as they could, but still be able to hear what was going on in the scrum.

"I've said before that I am not talking about the drug allegations," said Coach Jones.

"Mr. Mayor! Mr. Mayor!" A reporter waved the microphone in his face. "Today, an investigation has linked you to improper use of your office. Did you use your staff and influence as mayor to pay for new uniforms for Loyola?"

Coach Jones's face went red. Almost purple. Then he exhaled, forced a smile and rolled his eyes. "My office issued a reply to those charges earlier today. It was sent to all of the media organizations. I have nothing to add to that, other than the fact that Mr. Mather is a backstabbing little rat!"

"Mr. Mayor, can you answer these charges? Mr. Mather has provided us with copies of requests for funding for Loyola's new uniforms that were printed on letterhead from the mayor's office. We also understand you had your staff calling on residents, on behalf of the mayor's office, to donate to the football team. Do you not feel that's a conflict of interest — that you can't simply use the mayor's office as a way to try to fund your hobby?"

"This is ludicrous!" The red face returned in full force. "I have done nothing wrong! And you call this a *hobby*? Really? Ask these kids if they think football is a hobby. This witch hunt is all organized by you bloodsuckers in the media! You can't stand the fact that some working-class guy from the suburbs is now the mayor of this city. You'll do anything to drag me down. Fine. I get that. But don't you dare drag down these kids. Not because they're going to get some new jerseys and helmets. The nerve of you people!"

And, as the reporters called his name over and over, Bob Jones stormed off. Right toward the parking lot. More reporters surrounded him as he tried to get into his SUV.

"Please give me some space!" the mayor cried.

After the rest of the team had gone inside the dressing room and the coach had raced off in his SUV, Vijay and Maurice were left alone on the sidelines with only a few parents and fans still waiting in the stands behind them. Vijay looked over to Maurice. "I guess it looks like our post-game team talk has been postponed."

"It certainly does," came a voice from behind them. It came from Mr. DeAngelis.

"Now, you boys left a message that you wanted to talk to me after the game? I'm here. By the way, fine performances from both of you. Still weird watching from the stands, though."

"Yes, we needed to talk," said Maurice. "It's about Coach Jones."

"I figured. But it's a tall order. I mean, so much stuff out there, but none of it proven. Even with the picture he has excuses for everything. And he's the mayor."

"Yes, he reminds us of that every minute he coaches us," Vijay sighed.

"It's out of control, it's all about me this and me that with Coach Jones," said Maurice. "We're winning football games, but we're getting killed in practice. Every practice starts with some speech from the coach about how he's the greatest man ever and how everyone is out to get him. And I think it could get worse, too."

"And we just have to take it because he's the coach," said Vijay.

Coach DeAngelis touched his chin, looked upward, and then his eyes brightened. "But, *do* you have to take it? Guys, I think you're going about this all wrong. Maybe it isn't about proving Coach Jones has done drugs. Maybe it's about showing that he simply can't coach a football team anymore."

CHAPTER 15
WOLVERINES

Maurice and his mother joined the sea of blue football shirts and sweatshirts that surrounded the stadium. Maurice looked up and over the crowd, toward the stadium which towered over all of them.

"My God, Mom, it's bigger than I imagined. I mean, we've seen it on TV, but, in real life . . . it's just nuts."

"*Oui*, Maurice." His mother held a blue and yellow pom-pom in one hand and her son's arm with the other. "It is the biggest football stadium in all of the United States, no?"

"It holds more than 100,000 people."

The sight of the stadium, surrounded by football fans, permeated by the smell of popcorn, hot dogs, and stale beer, had brought Maurice back to life. He had emerged from the Detroit–Ann Arbor express bus feeling as if his eyes were going to sink right back inside of his skull.

He hadn't gotten much sleep; neither had his mom. They had planned to get some rest on the red-eye bus from Toronto to Detroit, but the bus smelled of stale corn chips and urine. And, the engine was loud. As they headed south on the 401, the bus lurched and jumped and bumped. The passenger behind them was listening to death metal at full blast on his headphones, and the sound bleeding out only made it even harder for Maurice or his mom to get any sleep. When the driver announced to his passengers that they were nearing the Ambassador Bridge and the American border, Maurice felt as if he hadn't got any sleep at all.

A security officer came onto the bus at the border, and Maurice's mom handed him their passports.

"My brother plays for the Wolverines," Maurice said.

The guard looked at the passports again, and read aloud, "Dumars. Dumars. Dumars. Never heard of any Dumars playing for the Wolverines. Anyways, all good. Enjoy your trip."

After a half-hour at the border, the bus rolled into downtown Detroit; the sky was purple-red, as it was only lightly kissed by the rising sun. Maurice and his mom found a bench at the bus station, near a security post, and laid next to their suitcases. Maurice had set the alarm on his phone for 8:30 a.m.; it allowed them to be up in time to catch the Ann Arbor bus, check in at the motel, and be at the stadium in plenty of time for the noon kickoff.

Maurice and his mom pushed through the stadium gate, flashing their tickets.

"Section 20. Let's go to section 20," said Maurice's mom.

They went up a few flights of stairs and then out toward

their seats. To Maurice, it looked like the seats went on forever. The field was so bright and beautiful and green, with the yellow M right in the middle. Some of the Michigan players, in blue and yellow, were jogging on the field or standing on the nearby sideline. On the other side were the white-and-green uniformed players of Michigan State, the Spartans.

Two state rivals. Both undefeated so far this season. In the far corner of the stadium, a group of green-sweatered Michigan State fans huddled together.

The crowd filled in around Maurice and his mom.

"There he is!" His mom pointed to the field excitedly.

Maurice saw player number 28 warming up for Michigan. That was Fabien's number. Maurice's mom waved frantically, but in such a massive sea of humanity it would have been almost impossible for Fabien to see her from his spot on the field.

The stadium was now three-quarters full, and there was a roar when number 32 jogged onto the field. Archie Anderson. When he crouched over to stretch, the crowd cheered. When he burst into a sprint, they roared.

It was already deafeningly loud, and kickoff was still more than a half-hour away.

Maurice and his mom were in a section that was now almost filled with howling fans. The person next to Maurice had painted his face blue and gold. Even his hair was dyed blue. The woman next to him wore an inflatable blue-and-yellow University of Michigan helmet that made her head seem like it belonged to some creature out of a comic book.

And, then, the noise stopped. Dead.

Archie Anderson was no longer running. He was on the turf, clutching his knee. The Michigan coaching staff and trainers ran onto the field. They helped Archie to his feet.

The star running back went down again.

"Nooooooo!!!" yelled Blue-Gold face.

A cart drove onto the field. Archie was laid on the flat back, and the vehicle slowly made its way toward the Michigan dressing room.

The roar that had been building from the crowd came to an abrupt end. Now, all was silent. Maurice could hear the breathing of the fans all around him.

"If the cart comes out, it means the player is hurt, bad," he whispered to his mom. "It means he can't walk off the field on his own."

"Maurice, your mother wasn't born yesterday," she hissed back. "I know what it means!"

As the cart disappeared into the tunnel, Maurice heard the whispers from the fans around him.

"There goes our season."

"Disaster."

"It's bad. It's really bad."

The teams went to their dressing rooms as kickoff time neared. At noon, the teams returned to the field, through the tunnels that led from the dressing room. The stadium was filled. And that was when the PA announcer's voice boomed:

"Starting at running back for Michigan, Fabien Dumars."

It was like music to Maurice's ears. Judging from previous games, Maurice had only expected to see his brother play three or four downs. But whoa, The Streak was starting!

"Crap!" said the woman with the helmet-head. She turned to Blue-Gold Face. "Fred, who is this guy?"

"Some nobody," said Blue-Gold face. "We are so doomed. He's the freshman running back. He's hardly played. And, well, he's from Canada."

"Canada?" cried Helmet Head. "They play football there? Why doesn't this guy play hockey?"

"Don't say a word, Maurice," his mom whispered into his ear.

The crowd cheered as Michigan State kicked off, and Michigan got the ball first. All eleven Michigan players clapped their hands in unison and then lined up for the first-down snap. Fabien was directly behind the quarterback. The ball was snapped and the quarterback put the ball in Fabien's hands.

Fabien was tackled three yards behind the line of scrimmage.

The crowd groaned. Blue-face swore. Helmet Head covered her eyes.

On the next play, the quarterback threw a short pass to Fabien. He dropped the ball. There was a smattering of boos from the crowd.

"Canada! Why did we try to find a player in Canada?!" Helmet Head bleated.

Two plays later, Michigan punted the ball to Michigan State. After an eight-play drive, Michigan State was able to kick a field goal to take a 3–0 lead.

Then Michigan got the ball back. And on the first play,

Fabien was again stopped behind the line of scrimmage. He lost two yards on the play.

"Canadians can only run backward!" yelled Blue-Gold Face.

"He's terrible!" cried Helmet Head.

Michigan's players emerged from the huddle. It was second down and twelve yards to go. The quarterback went back like he was going to pass. But Fabien remained next to him. Then the quarterback made a quick hand-off to Fabien.

Fabien plunged ahead. He smashed into a Michigan State defender — and didn't go down. He bounced to the left and kept running. He extended his arm and pushed away another would-be tackler.

Now the crowd was roaring. So loud. Like a thousand jets landing at the airport.

Fabien broke another tackle, cut back toward the inside of the field. The end zone was only twenty yards away. He accelerated again, outrunning the last Spartan who had a shot at bringing him down. Fabien ran through the end zone, and then laid the ball down. He thrust both hands in the air.

Blue-Gold Face and Helmet Head hugged each other and cheered. In a corner of the stadium, the band started to play, horns swaying back and forth.

Maurice embraced his mom so tightly, that her feet rose up off the ground.

Maurice then turned toward Blue-Gold Face, Helmet Head, and the rest of the fans in his row.

"That's my big brother!" he yelled.

★★★

FROM SCRUB TO STREAK

SPORTS NEWS SERVICE — The Michigan
Wolverines boast the best running back in the
country. But today, a running back from another
country did more than just fill in for him.

Canadian Fabien Dumars — known as 'The
Streak' when he played high-school football in
Toronto — was thrust into action after NCAA
leading rusher Archie Anderson was injured in
the warm-up ahead of the Wolverines' must-win
game against Michigan State.

By the end of the game, Dumars showed he
can carry the Wolverines if Anderson's injury is
serious enough to keep him out for an extended
period. Dumars scampered for 175 yards and
three touchdowns as the Wolverines beat their
cross-state rivals 28–17.

On the Wolverines' first drive of the game,
Dumars was stopped for a loss and then dropped
a pass that hit him in the hands. On the team's
second drive, he heard boos when he was stopped
for a loss. But in front of an anxious crowd, the
Wolverines called the Statue of Liberty play on
second and 12. Quarterback Jay Lovitz went back
as if to pass, then handed the ball to Dumars, who
then scampered 82 yards to the end zone.

CHAPTER 16
MEETING A HERO

Maurice's phone buzzed. There was a text message from Vijay.

> GR8 GAME! TELL FABIEN HE'S THE BEST! HAVE U SEEN THIS? COACH JONES!

There was a link at the end of the message. Maurice clicked it.

MAYOR DRUNK IN PUBLIC

TORONTO (CP) — Embattled Toronto Mayor Bob Jones, already accused of drug use and improper use of his office, has another public-relations disaster on his hand.

On Friday night, less than two hours after

coaching his Loyola high school football team to a 35–7 win over Our Lady of Fatima, the mayor was spotted on Danforth Avenue, with a bottle of vodka in his hand.

A camera-phone video obtained by this news agency appears to show the mayor swearing. He also appears to say something about "media leeches" and "that son of a bitch DeAngelis." It has been confirmed that Loyola teacher Massimo DeAngelis was a former assistant coach on the football team, but was removed.

The school board is investigating the conduct of the mayor, who continues to coach his team despite allegations he used office staff and resources to help raise funds for the Loyola team.

As of late Friday, the mayor continued to be the hot topic among late-night talk shows in Canada and the United States. A source told CP that the mayor has received an invitation to appear on the Late Night Show on CBS, which is taped in Hollywood.

"The mayor's antics are seen by the public in two ways," said University of Toronto civics professor Dr. Harold Lantos. "For many, he is an embarrassment to the city. But for others, he is seen as bringing international attention to the city of Toronto."

While Jones's office would not comment on this latest issue, his cousin and campaign manager, Nick Jones, said that being drunk is not a crime.

"He did what a lot of people do on Friday nights, and that's let off steam," said Nick Jones. "If you say the mayor should resign because he drinks on a Friday night, then you should also quit your job if you've had a drink on the weekend. Am I right?"

Meanwhile, Toronto Police say they continue to chase several tips as they hunt for Ramanan Panesar's killer. The trail had gone cold, but police say they have received "many tips" since the public release of the photo, which appears to show then-councilor Jones with the slain drug dealer. Jones continues to deny the photo's authenticity.

Maurice's mom tapped him on the shoulder. They were waiting in a lounge beneath the stadium that was reserved for the family and closest friends of the University of Michigan players and coaches. The doors to the lounge opened, and through them walked Fabien. And then next to him, on crutches, hopped Archie Anderson.

Maurice and his mom each hugged Fabien.

"What a game!" said Maurice.

"So this is your brother you were telling me about?" asked Archie.

"Yeah," said Fabien. "The one who's gonna break all my school records."

Maurice bit his lip before speaking. "Fabien, I'm so glad for you, but Mr. Anderson . . ."

"Archie."

"Okay, um, Archie, I'm sorry you got hurt."

"It's okay," smiled Archie. "Trainer and the doc think it's

just a sprain. I'll be out a couple of weeks. But your brother did awesome. I see him in practice every day, I knew if he got a chance, he'd be fine. What a great day for him."

"And Archie should be back when we play the big game against Ohio State in a few weeks," Fabien grinned.

"I wish my team was like that," Maurice sighed. "I mean, you guys support each other. You cheer for each other. On our team, the other running back only bothers to talk to me so he can put me down."

"Football can't work like that," said Archie, shaking his head. "We have to support each other. It's all about the team. You help the team have success, and the individual stuff comes after. We're a family. We've got each other's backs."

Archie patted Maurice on the shoulder. "Now, can I ask you a question?"

"Sure."

"What's it like playing for the Crack Coach? They made fun of him on all the late-night shows last week! He's like, the most famous mayor in any city ever! And you play for that guy!"

Maurice groaned. *Even in Michigan, I can't get away from Coach Jones*, he thought. "Did my brother mention that I might break his records?"

Seeing the look on Maurice's face, Archie Anderson laughed so hard that he almost fell off his crutches. Fabien had to put his arm around Archie so his teammate could keep steady.

"No, seriously," Archie said after he steadied himself. "Next time you come down to Michigan, can you do me a favour?"

"What?" said Maurice.

"Bring me Bob Jones's autograph! I mean, that would be sick!"

Maurice's mom cleared her throat. "Archie, may I ask you a question?"

Archie turned his attention away from Maurice. "Yes, Mrs. Dumars."

"Where are you from?"

"Detroit."

"Would you be proud if your city's mayor was famous because he was doing all the wrong things? I would much rather that our mayor was famous because our city was recognized as a great place to live."

Archie smiled. "Honestly, I don't pay that much attention to what a mayor does. Or a president. I haven't voted yet. But I do know that there were Detroit mayors who were kicked out of office. That was on the news when I was younger. But they don't put it on the news if the mayor is doing a good job, do they?"

"No, they don't," sighed Mrs. Dumars. "That's a good point. You have to be a buffoon to make news. To be famous. If you're a sensible leader and make good decisions, no one seems to care. I will tell you this: Maurice and Fabien's father — God rest his soul — and I came from Haiti, and it was run by a dictator. A crazy man. I have seen what happens when someone who is clearly unfit to lead is not challenged."

Archie nodded. "I guess you're right, but your mayor isn't really evil. He's just, well, entertaining."

"That's the way most people might see it — if they

don't have to live in his city." Mrs. Dumars shook her head.

Maurice spoke up. "I might be able get you that auto-graph. But I need something in return, Archie."

"If it's not against the NCAA rules, I can do it. If I do anything that involves money, I'm off the team."

"Just a simple trade," said Maurice.

"Okay, what's the offer?"

CHAPTER 17

SPECIAL DELIVERY

SPECIAL BULLETIN FROM NEWS TALK RADIO

This morning, the legal team representing former Bob Jones press flack Chuck Mather issued the following statement.

"Charles Mather will no longer speak to the media regarding allegations of improper use of office funds and resources directed by Mayor Bob Jones. Mr. Mather apologizes for any distress this may have caused the mayor. Mr. Mather wants to assure the media that he was mistaken; that any time spent by staff to work on raising funds for the Loyola football program was done on their own time, after office hours, and strictly on a volunteer basis."

NEWS TALK Radio has attempted to contact Mr. Mather, but we have been told that he is not in Toronto at the moment, that he's on an extended trip outside of the country.

The brown delivery van backed to the sidelines of the practice field. The driver switched off the ignition, jumped out of the cab, and opened the two back doors.

"Gentlemen!" Coach Jones called to the players who were standing on the field. "If you'd all grab a box and just lay them here on the field."

Coach Jones clapped his hands as the boys began unloading the cargo.

Throughout the school day that Monday, Maurice hadn't been able to keep his thoughts on his studies. Math equations were just numbers with x's and n's. His social studies class discussed how the latest accusations about Coach Jones, allegations he was drunk in public, might sway the school-board vote. Once again, the teacher reminded the class that Bob Jones had not been charged with a crime, and hadn't even been arrested. But Maurice didn't have anything to say. He was thinking about what he was going to do after that afternoon's football practice. He was going to have to face his rival.

And now practice had begun — with the unloading of a van. The boxes were all stacked on the grass. Coach Jones blew his whistle.

"Everyone line up." He smiled. "No, don't worry, this is going to be fun. You guys may have all heard about the lies that the media are trying to dig up on me, just because I thought this fine football program deserved new jerseys.

Well, I've had my lawyers send the media organizations a letter that they are no longer welcome at our practices. You kids are nowhere near eighteen, and they can't just keep coming here and filming you without my permission. Now, for the jerseys. Well, here they are!"

Coach Jones hunched over a box, and his arms reached down and ripped the flaps open. The tape holding the box together was no match for the coach's show of strength.

He yanked out a red jersey with a bright number 81 on it. It was Vijay's number. The coach walked over to Vijay and handed him the shirt.

"That's going to look great!" said the coach. "Now, gentlemen, please, help yourselves."

The boys walked over to the boxes and tore them open like it was Christmas morning. There were more red jerseys. There were red helmets that sparkled when they caught the orange rays of the late-fall-afternoon sun. The boys pulled jerseys out of the boxes, looking for their numbers. Some were the home reds, while others were bright white shirts for the road games.

Maurice found his number 28 in both shirts. He also found Vijay's white 81. *Damn, the new jerseys look sharp*, Maurice thought.

But Coach Jones interrupted Maurice's thoughts with another shrill blow of the whistle.

"Okay, guys, we need to prep for our next game of the season. It was supposed to be our week off, but we have to play Pope John Paul II. It's our make-up game from earlier. We are going to show that, even shorthanded, we'll be impossible to beat."

Shorthanded? wondered Maurice.

Coach Jones's smile disappeared. "I see by the looks on your faces that you are all wondering what I mean when I say 'shorthanded.' Well, here it is . . ."

Coach Jones pulled an envelope out of his jacket pocket.

"I thought about doing this in private with the player involved. But then I thought, no. This should done in front of all of you. We are a team. So, discipline should be administered in front of the whole team."

"Looks like André might finally get what's coming to him for all of the talking he does in practice," Vijay whispered to Maurice.

Coach Jones took a deep breath. "We all respect what Mr. DeAngelis did as a coach of this team. But he isn't a coach anymore. But one of our players didn't respect the fact that Coach DeAngelis decided that he didn't want to be with us anymore. Maurice didn't go to the dressing room after our game — he was talking to Mr. DeAngelis right on the field."

Coach Jones wiped his sleeve across his brow as his face turned red.

"So, it's pretty clear to me that someone is trying to undermine me. I thought all the leeches were in the press. But hell, there seems to be one on my team!"

Coach Jones fixed his eyes on Maurice.

"So, Maurice. Why sneak behind my back like this?"

"B-b-but Coach, it wasn't like that," Maurice stammered. "Mr. DeAngelis is still a teacher at the school, and he didn't leave, you got rid of him . . ."

"SHUT UP!" screamed Jones. "I may have been the one to make the final decision, but DeAngelis made it quite clear he didn't want to be here!"

Vijay's hand shot up.

"Yes, Vijay, what is it?" snapped Coach Jones.

"I was there, too. I talked to Coach DeAngelis, too. And he's a teacher of mine, as well. I just don't think you should single out Maurice when I was there, too."

The coach rubbed his chin. "I know you were there, Vijay. But you don't have to set an example for the team like Maurice has to."

"Why don't *you* set an example?" Maurice grumbled in the coach's direction.

"What? WHAT?" screamed Bob Jones.

"You heard me, Coach. *I'm* not getting drunk after games. *I'm* not swearing at the reporters. And *I* don't smoke crack."

"SHUT UP!" Coach Jones howled. "You've seen how I treat people who are loyal to me, huh? You all got new jerseys and helmets. Now, you'll all see what happens to people who try to screw me over!

"Maurice, you get this straight. You ain't playing on Friday. You're suspended. You're some poor kid who gets his shot and now thinks he's bigger than anyone else. Well, you can spend the rest of the practice running laps."

Maurice was frozen in place as Coach Jones glared at him.

"NOW!" Jones's voice boomed. "Give those laps to me now, Maurice, or god help me I will drive to Michigan and tell the coach there that Fabien was Ronny's partner! I'll ruin Fabien!"

Maurice felt one foot move in front of the other. Soon, his legs and lungs were burning. If he slowed down, Coach Jones commanded him to speed up.

Finally, Maurice corkscrewed into the ground, panting.

"Leave him there," he heard Jones command the rest of the team. Maurice lay on the grass, staring at the darkening sky, until he heard three blasts of the coach's whistle — the signal that practice was over.

Vijay sprinted over to Maurice and crouched down. "Look, I tried to take the blame, too — but because of this whole Ronny picture thing, he won't punish me. I know that's the reason."

Maurice didn't speak. Or couldn't. He used his last drops of remaining strength to sit up, and then he put his palms down on the grass so he could push himself into a standing position. He staggered into the dressing room. It was silent. But through all the pain and fatigue, Maurice remembered his mission. He dialed the combination on his locker, opened the door, and picked up the bag that lay within.

He then sat down — but not next to Vijay. Instead, he plunked himself right by André.

"What the hell?" André said. "Look, if you think I ratted you out to the coach, I didn't. I don't like you, but I'm not the kind of guy who tells tall tales."

"I'm not here to accuse you of anything," Maurice whispered. "I'm here to make you an offer."

"What's that? To do your laps with you? Dude, you are so far in the doghouse you should have a tag."

Why does André make it so hard for me? Maurice thought. *I just want to punch him. Okay, Maurice. Breathe. BREATHE.*

"Man, what's with the Darth Vader sounds?" André said. He looked around as their other teammates were leaving the showers, getting dressed, and heading out. "Look, you got something to say to me? Say it. I've got better things to do. I've got to get my rest, because it looks like I'm starting on Friday."

Maurice thought about picking up the bag and just walking out, with his football gear still on. Instead, he nudged the bag toward André, and then slowly undid the zipper. The bag parted open. There was a blue football jersey in the bag. "For you."

"Really, you got me your brother's jersey? Lame! You think I care about him or you?"

"Look at it, André. It's not my brother's jersey. It's Archie Anderson's jersey. He gave it to me. He signed it on the number in the front. And now I'm giving it to you."

André went silent. For once, there were no smart remarks or insults. Finally, just one word passed his lips: "Why?"

"Why? Look, I got to meet Archie on the weekend. He was hurt, he's going to miss some games. And was he mad? He didn't show it. He was happy that my brother got into the game and helped the team win. He showed me what being a teammate is about."

"Wow. I mean, this could be worth a lot of money one day. Archie Anderson is going to be a star."

"This morning I'd just planned to give this jersey to you as a peace offering or something. But after all that went down today, I'm just going to say this. I don't care what Bob Jones does to me or why I'm not playing. I just wanted to tell you to go get 'em on Friday."

"Even after everything I said to you . . . all season?"

"You said stuff to me before?" Maurice got up from his seat. "Funny, I seem to have forgotten it all."

CHAPTER 18
THE PLAN

Maurice sat on the park bench next to Vijay. The sun was setting. He looked at the playground that sat empty in front of him and his friend. There was a raised bar; chains dangled from it. At one time it had been a swing set, but the seats and saddles were gone. Behind that was a paved court; bare backboards towered over it. The basketball hoops, like the swings, were nowhere to be seen. Everything in the park looked as if something was missing.

"So, I guess that's it, then." Maurice looked at his phone.

"No way, there's got to be another way," Vijay said.

The latest story was on the screen of Maurice's phone.

Vijay looked over Maurice's shoulder at the screen display. "What does 'in camera' mean?"

"I think it's when they have a private talk and kick all the reporters out," Maurice said. "We talked about it in social studies class."

SCHOOL BOARD BACKS JONES

By Colleen Nakamura

The Catholic School Board has rejected calls to remove Mayor Bob Jones as coach of the Loyola Catholic High School junior football team.

After a two-hour in camera meeting, the school board voted 10–2 against the removal of Jones as the coach. But it did vote 10–2 in favour of having trustee Jimmy Costa attend all remaining Loyola High School football games to monitor the conduct of the coach.

The Chair of the board, Shelly West, said that while reports of the mayor's conduct were "troubling," there were no allegations of misconduct brought forward by any of the students.

"In the end, all we had was an allegation from a teacher and we felt that the evidence that he gave may have been affected by a personal issue between him and Bob Jones," said West. "But we understand that there are serious, but unproven, allegations about the mayor, so Trustee Costa will monitor the situation and report back to the board."

Mayor Jones, reached at his office, said he was "always confident" he would prevail.

"Look, if they want to babysit me, that's fine. I've got nothing to hide. I just want to win some football games and help some kids. The leeches don't understand that, because the only people they ever want to help are themselves."

Vijay and Maurice stared at the screen for another moment, then, finally, Vijay changed the subject. "How are your feet?"

"Sore," said Maurice. "In fact, they hurt more than they have after any game we've played this year. I lost count of how many laps I did. That's three practices in a row he's done this to me."

"Okay, but we gotta do something about Coach Jones. We need to show that we've had enough."

"How?" asked Maurice. "You saw the news. The school board is backing the mayor."

"Yeah, and I've met this Costa guy," Vijay said. "He's like, as bad as my dad when it comes to not seeing anything that Bob Jones does wrong. I think that if Bob Jones killed a guy live on TV, my dad might still vote for him. Same with Costa."

"Well, what do we have here?" came a voice from up the park path. "Look at you two sorry excuses for football players."

"André?" cried Vijay. "What is *he* doing here?"

Maurice raised his hand. "It's cool. I texted him."

"You two text now?" Vijay looked stunned.

André walked out of the shadows and into the yellow glow of the park lights. "So, you wanted to talk to me?"

"Yeah," Maurice said. "I think I'm gonna quit."

André shrugged. "So, you're in the coach's doghouse and you're just going to give up?"

"Yeah, I just wanted to tell you so you're ready, that you don't hear it from Coach Jones."

"For three practices I've watched you doing lap after lap until you almost collapse. That's not cool. Our coach has called us lazy. He's threatened us. And no one is doing anything about it." André sighed and shoved his hands into his pockets. "Look, it's like this. I was angry when you got here. And it wasn't until you gave me that shirt that I realized exactly why I was angry. I wasn't angry because I thought the coach was playing favourites, it was because you're so damn good. I thought I'd come in and play most of the downs, and then you come in and, well, look at the yards you pile up. So yeah, I was being selfish. It's not fair, when you think about it. So many of us just want one shot to make it, to get a chance to play in the big time. And your family, well, it's gonna get two shots. Your brother, and you."

"But it wasn't just you giving Vijay and me a hard time, it was the whole team," said Maurice.

"So, you think we were all cool just rolling through goose crap? You thought we were all just fine with it? You thought we were all just fine with being called fat and lazy? The extra laps? The puking? Sure, that's what I call a fun way to spend my after-school time. Yeah, we saw you as the coach's pets. So when the coach took it out on us, we took it out on you." André paused and sighed again. "Look, you might think this is weird, but over the last couple of days you've taught me a bit about what it's like to be on a team. That means we should look out for each other."

Vijay interrupted. "How? The trustees are in Bob Jones's back pocket!"

145

André smiled. "So?"

"What do you mean, 'so?'"

"Didn't you see what they said? No student came forward. But what if *we* did?"

"No one would believe us."

"Wait, Vijay," Maurice said. "Didn't Mr. DeAngelis tell us we needed to show that Bob Jones couldn't coach us? We have more media at our games than some CFL teams. He can kick the reporters out of our practices, but they can still come to our games."

"So, we could use that," André said, looking thoughtful. "We could do something, as a team. And I've got an idea. We can see if it works. If it doesn't, Maurice, I totally get it if you want to quit. I couldn't stand a whole season of being treated like you've been for the last few days. But hear me out. You guys do your part, I'll talk to the rest of the guys on the team."

CHAPTER 19
THE SHOW

Maurice sat next to his mother in the front row of the stands. He waved to Mr. Panesar, who was sitting a few rows up, next to school trustee Jimmy Costa. Next to the bespectacled spectator sat the school principal.

Maurice adjusted his tie. He wore his best (and only) suit jacket and then an open-zippered winter coat over top. Mrs. Dumars insisted that, even though her son was suspended for the game, that he look like a young professional. Maurice was not going to argue with her.

It was a cold night, below the freezing mark. Maurice thought that he'd much rather be keeping warm by running around rather than sitting in the stands with a few dozen spectators.

On the other side of the field were the lights coming from the TV cameras. Just as Vijay predicted, the Toronto media was out to see Mayor Bob Jones coach another game.

The players from Pope John Paul II were out on the field, doing their stretches, running their sprints. The Loyola players hadn't come out of their dressing room yet.

Finally, as if they were members of a rock band making the audience wait to see the encore, the Loyola players dashed out in their bright red shirts.

André and Vijay were at the front of the pack of players.

"Here it comes," Maurice whispered to his mom.

"Wait and see, wait and see," she said.

Instead of going into their warm-up routine on the field, the players kept in a line and continued to jog behind André and Vijay. They moved all the way across the width of the field, past their team bench, and then into the stands. The players climbed up the stairs, all looking for places to sit. One by one, the red-clad footballers found open spots on the benches. They pulled off their helmets and wedged them between their knees.

Bob Jones hadn't seen it happen. He was too busy looking at the cameras and reporters on the other side of the field. He had stopped to smile and wave and get his picture taken. He gave a thumbs-up pose as flashes popped.

But when the reporters began pointing at the stands, Bob Jones whirled and saw what his players had done. Some of the media began crossing the field so they could get a better look at what was happening.

Bob Jones followed as fast as he could, which wasn't really very fast at all. So the cameras were rolling and the reporters had their notebooks open by the time Jones got to the stands.

He roared at the players. "What are you doing? What is the meaning of this?"

It was André who stood up. "Sorry, Coach. We had a team vote. We're not playing tonight."

"What?!" the coach took the baseball cap off his head and flung it onto the ground. "Is this some kind of joke? Do you know what happens? You? André? All season you gripe about not playing, then you get the chance to start — AND THEN YOU PULL THIS CRAP? That referee over there is going to award a forfeit win to those guys over there! Do you want to lose?"

"It's just one loss," André said. "We'll still be in first place, we'll still be in the playoffs. But we need to send a message, Coach."

"Message! Do you know who I am? I'm your mayor! I'm your coach! I *made* you guys!"

Now it was Vijay's turn to stand and talk. "That's where you're wrong. You didn't *make* any of us. We are who we are. But you do a lot of other things for us."

Another player stood up. "Like calling us fat asses."

Another. "Like making us roll through crap."

Another. "You play favourites."

One more. "And the team is always in the news. But not because of football. Because you're breaking rules to get us stuff or trying to tell everyone how awesome you are."

And then it was Maurice's turn to stand. "You take credit for everything. You take credit for my brother's success and he's doing just fine without you."

Vijay spoke again. "And you were with my cousin. You weren't trying to save him. Come on, Mr. Jones. I can see that."

Mr. Panesar sat, wide-eyed, as his son spoke.

Vijay turned to a TV reporter with a video camera. "We won't play for Coach Jones anymore. He has a problem."

"I don't have a problem!" Bob Jones screamed. "Just because I have a drink here and there doesn't mean I have a problem! Maybe I've made some other mistakes, but I'm only human."

Maurice jumped out of the first row of the stands, onto the grass, and walked right up to his coach.

"That's right, Coach. You *are* only human. But to us, you don't act like a human at all. Look at what you've become. You're angry all the time. You torture us at practice. Even pro players wouldn't take this. I talked to Fabien, and he said he couldn't believe what he sees on the TV."

Vijay spoke again. "My dad believed in you. My family wasted months campaigning for you and backing you and defending you."

Vijay pivoted and stared straight at his father. "Dad, you're here at this game tonight because the guy from the school board is here to monitor Coach Jones. You've always been right about one thing: we've needed a change in this neighbourhood, in this city. But you've put so much faith in Bob Jones that you can't see he's not the man you think he is. Look, football was the one thing that kept Ronny in check; it was the last thing he really loved. And I finally figured out why. A team is like a family. We might not get along all of the time — actually, not most of the time — but in the end we look out for each other. And I'm sorry, Dad, that's what I've got to do here."

Mr. Panesar stood up.

"Dad?" Vijay asked, looking surprised.

"My son is right, Bob. We did believe in you. And we kept believing in you. Even when all the proof was in our faces. Maybe it's time to stop believing in you. Why, Bob, why? Why were you with my nephew that night? Why do you keep making excuses?"

The flashes were going off like strobe lights. The cameras were all pointed at the mayor.

"To HELL with all of you! I'll crush you all! You can HAVE your stinking team! I don't have a problem! I've done NOTHING wrong! NOTHING!"

Bob Jones picked up the baseball cap he'd thrown, then threw it down again. He stomped on it, grinding the fabric into the grass. He then turned around and stormed off toward the parking lot. The reporters chased him like a pack of wolves.

"I think he just quit," André said.

The school principal dashed out of the stands and chased after the reporters and Bob Jones.

Then Jimmy Costa stood up. "Excuse me! I am James Costa, I am your trustee! I have taken note of everything that has gone on here, and it will go into my report to the school board. It looks like I will recommend that, without a coach, the Loyola football program be cancelled for the season."

"What!" came cries from the players and chatter broke out amongst everyone in the stands.

Maurice raised up both of his hands and the noise immediately lessened.

"Yes?" Jimmy Costa pointed at him.

"You don't need to cancel the program! Not if we have a new coach!" He shouted to be sure that everyone heard.

"And who would want to do that?" asked Jimmy Costa.

"I would."

The voice came from a man who had been standing quietly behind the stands. He walked into Jimmy Costa's field of vision.

"I'd love to coach again," said Mr. DeAngelis. "I've been an assistant for a long time, and I'd be honoured to coach these boys."

The boys roared their approval.

Coach DeAngelis checked his watch. "Maurice, you'd better get your uniform and pads on. They're stashed away in the athletic office. Go! I believe, by league rules, we still have about five minutes before the referee declares a forfeit. So, gentlemen, can I suggest you get out of the stands and start warming up? I mean, you're all suited up, right?"

"I knew it was a good idea to let Mr. DeAngelis in on your plan," Maurice's mom said with a smile.

"Yes, and that's why you decided to call him," Maurice said and then dashed off toward the school to change.

"For sure," Mrs. Dumars called after him. "I don't think anyone can suspend me or make me do laps!"

The next morning, Toronto's tabloid newspaper ran a photo of Bob Jones walking alone across the football field. The stands rose behind him in the background.

"I QUIT"
By Desiree Williamson, Staff Reporter

Bob Jones has finally decided to quit his volunteer role as the coach of the Loyola Catholic High School football team.

But it didn't happen because Jones was responding to pressure from constituents and council to quit football so he could spend more hours focused on his job as the mayor of Toronto. In front of a legion of cameras and reporters, the players on his football team staged a protest, refusing to go on the field ahead of their scheduled game against Pope John Paul II High School.

When Jones realized what was happening, he announced that he's quitting the football post — and then stormed off the field.

Teacher and former assistant coach Massimo DeAngelis, who was on-site, was appointed head coach minutes after Jones's departure. Under his leadership, the Loyola team came out with a 38–10 win.

Later, Jones spoke to reporters via telephone conference.

"I apologize for the manner in which I left the field," he said. "I'm a passionate guy, it's who I am, I wear my heart on my sleeve. I know the boys can win the city title. I built this team and they'll finish the job."

Even though the mayor had to be pushed out of

the coaching job by his team, he could still end up a political winner.

"Voters have very short memories," said York University political science professor Ira Goldstein. "We are still years away from another election, which will allow Jones's camp to change the message. They'll say that they listened to voters and Jones stepped away from football so he could focus on being the mayor. They know that, in a few short weeks, we'll all forget that the reason he quit was because his players wanted him out."

CHAPTER 20

THE RECORD

Maurice dashed toward the St. Peter's linebacker. He leaned forward, and the defending player was knocked to the ground. Maurice had successfully blocked the last man who had a legitimate shot to tackle the Loyola player with the ball cradled in his right arm. That player was Vijay.

Vijay saw that he had an open green field in front of him now that Maurice had made the big block. His feet carried him, faster, faster, toward the end zone. When he crossed the goal line, he felt like time had stopped. He thought about his dad, who had spent the last week driving all of the Bob Jones signs that were in the garage out to the local landfill site. And Vijay thought about Ronny, whose name he had scrawled in marker on each of his shoes.

The Loyola students roared as Vijay entered the end zone. Before he could even spike the ball, Maurice had caught up to him and picked him up in a mighty bear hug.

He looked up at the scoreboard. The score was now 27–14 for Loyola, with an extra point still to come. There were only thirty seconds left on the clock — the regional championship would be theirs.

Maurice put Vijay down and they looked at the Loyola fans. In the stands at Birchmount Stadium, way out in Scarborough on the eastern side of the Greater Toronto Area, the fans looked like they were so far away. Vijay had never played in a stadium this large before.

But compared to what Maurice had seen in Ann Arbor, Birchmount might as well have been the size of a postage stamp.

Vijay and Maurice were mobbed on the sideline by their teammates. After the embraces came handshakes from their coach. Coach DeAngelis wore a red Loyola ball cap and hoodie. He grinned from ear to ear.

"We're thirty seconds away from doing this," he said to Vijay and Maurice. "Enjoy it."

Vijay watched the clock tick down as the defence stopped the opposition's last-gasp attempts to move the ball.

Nearby on the sidelines, Maurice tapped André on the shoulder. There were now only five seconds left. St. Peter's had a third down and ten yards to go. There was no chance the opponents could make up the thirteen-point deficit.

"Come on," Maurice motioned André to follow him. They joined two other teammates who had edged near the orange vat of Gatorade. They nodded and, together, all four of them picked it up and held it high in the air. They carried it toward DeAngelis and then, before their coach could react, they dumped the icy contents over his head and shoulders. The cap was swept off DeAngelis's head by a wave of sticky cold orange sports drink. The players dropped the empty vat on the ground.

Coach DeAngelis laughed, and high-fived each of his players. The final gun sounded. The title game was over. As Coach Jones had predicted, Loyola won the title. But Coach Jones wasn't on the sidelines. He had been banned from all school activities.

The silver bowl was brought out to midfield, and the Loyola players gathered around it. They applauded when Coach DeAngelis hoisted it into the air. They cheered when he handed it to Maurice, who gave the bowl a kiss. It went to André, and then to every player on the squad.

Maurice looked into the crowd. He saw his mom, wearing a "Maurice Dumars is my son" T-shirt. Next to her, wearing a blue Michigan sweatshirt, was his brother. The Wolverines didn't have a game that weekend, so Fabien had come back home to watch his kid brother play.

Vijay also looked into the stands, searching for his mom and dad — and he smiled and waved when he spotted them. They were walking down the steps, looking for a way to make it onto the field.

"Heck of a touchdown, son," his dad smiled.

Fabien got up, walked down the stairs and met Maurice on the sideline.

"Good game, bro," said Fabien. "I was adding up your carries on my phone. I think you rushed for about 180 yards."

"Thanks."

"You would have got a lot more, too."

Coach DeAngelis walked over to Fabien. They shook hands.

"Yeah, maybe he could have got more," said DeAngelis. "But he can't hog the ball all game long. So, I have to make sure André, our other back over there, gets some carries, too. Together, they're like thunder and lightning! I want to make sure Maurice here isn't all burned out by the time he's eligible to go to Michigan, just like his big brother! After all, I've got to prep him. You have a couple of years now to go and set all the Michigan records, and then your kid brother is going to come up and break them."

Fabien smiled. "Really, Coach, nothing would make me happier."

Meanwhile, in the stadium parking lot, far away from the players, parents, and the fans, Mayor Jones stood and clapped. Even though he wasn't allowed near the Loyola football team or the stadium itself, the ban didn't extend to the parking lot. There were TV cameras all around him.

MAYOR REMAINS LOYOLA'S BIGGEST FAN
By Desiree Williamson

Toronto Mayor Bob Jones said he always wanted to see the Loyola Catholic High School football team win the city title. On Friday night, he got the chance to celebrate that championship.

But he didn't do it on the field. He did it from

the parking lot of Birchmount Stadium.

After the Toronto Catholic School Board ruled that the mayor could not be in the stadium for the final, he chose to be as close to the team as the law would allow. In fact, he rescheduled a scheduled dinner with the Premier of Ontario so he could be at the game.

Jones quit his volunteer role as the head coach of the Loyola team five weeks ago — after his players organized a public protest ahead of a league game.

"I could not be happier," Jones said. "I am not bitter. Why would I be bitter? Let me be clear: That was my team you all saw down there. I built that program. The kids all know who their real coach is. Me. And the team's success, well that's a lesson for everyone in Toronto. That team showed that I get results. I built that team, I made that team. I'm a winner. It was my decision to quit, don't forget that. I didn't have to. Sure, the kids were going through a tough time. So I made the sacrifice."

The mayor also defended his decision to move his meeting with the Premier.

"The Premier, she understands that a schedule may need to be rearranged. This was only supposed to be an informal meeting, anyway. Look, she has plenty of time to meet with me. After all, I am going to be mayor of this city for a long, long time."

Etobicoke4Life
Innocent! He'll always have my vote!

BikeRider66
Just another example of our messed-up city. People are still
out there who see our mayor as some kind of role model.
Embarrassing.

RIFLEMAN
Best mayor EVER

ReelDeelz
Mayor is a WINNER.

MrJohnWILD17
I fear for this city. I really do.